"Someone has cut the fuel line," Ryan announced, his voice echoing in the still air.

He took out his cell phone. No signal alert. He ground his teeth in frustration.

"Kiki, can you see if you have a signal?" He turned to find her staring transfixed at the car. The terrified expression on her lovely face sent concern arcing through him. He rushed to her side. "Kiki?"

"Would it have blown up if I'd started it?" she asked, her voice wobbly.

"Not likely. Whoever did this would have known there was no way we'd get in with the smell of fuel so strong."

"But if we hadn't smelled the fumes?" she insisted.

"Still unlikely, unless..."

"Unless?"

He shrugged. "Unless there was more tampering."

Books by Terri Reed

Love Inspired Suspense

Strictly Confidential
*Double Deception
Beloved Enemy
Her Christmas Protector
*Double Jeopardy
*Double Cross

*The McClains

Love Inspired

Love Comes Home
A Sheltering Love
A Sheltering Heart
A Time of Hope
Giving Thanks for Baby

TERRI REED

At an early age Terri Reed discovered the wonderful world of fiction and declared she would one day write a book. Now she is fulfilling that dream and enjoys writing for Steeple Hill Books. Her second book, *A Sheltering Love,* was a 2006 RITA® Award finalist and a 2005 National Reader's Choice Award finalist. Her book *Strictly Confidential,* book five of the FAITH AT THE CROSSROADS continuity series, took third place for the 2007 American Christian Fiction Writers Book of the Year Award. She is an active member of both Romance Writers of America and American Christian Fiction Writers. She resides in the Pacific Northwest with her college-sweetheart husband, two wonderful children and an array of critters. When not writing, she enjoys spending time with her family and friends, gardening and playing with her dogs.

You can write to Terri at P.O. Box 19555 Portland, OR 97280 or visit her on the Web at www.loveinspiredauthors.com or leave comments on her blog at ladiesofsuspense.blogspot.com.

Terri Reed
DOUBLE CROSS

Steeple
Hill®

Published by Steeple Hill Books™

STEEPLE HILL BOOKS

Steeple
Hill®

ISBN-13: 978-0-373-44305-5
ISBN-10:   0-373-44305-6

DOUBLE CROSS

Copyright © 2008 by Terri Reed

All rights reserved. Except for use in any review, the reproduction
or utilization of this work in whole or in part in any form by any
electronic, mechanical or other means, now known or hereafter
invented, including xerography, photocopying and recording, or in
any information storage or retrieval system, is forbidden without
the written permission of the editorial office, Steeple Hill Books,
233 Broadway, New York, NY 10279 U.S.A.

This is a work of fiction. Names, characters, places and incidents are
either the product of the author's imagination or are used fictitiously, and
any resemblance to actual persons, living or dead, business establishments,
events or locales is entirely coincidental.

This edition published by arrangement with Steeple Hill Books.

® and TM are trademarks of Steeple Hill Books, used under license.
Trademarks indicated with ® are registered in the United States Patent
and Trademark Office, the Canadian Trade Marks Office and in other
countries.

www.SteepleHill.com

Printed in U.S.A.

Have I not commanded you? Be strong and courageous! Do not tremble or be dismayed, for the Lord your God is with you wherever you go.

—*Joshua* 1:9

To my family: without your love and support
I'd be a basket case.

To Leah and Melissa: as always,
you pick me up when I fall down. Thanks!

ONE

An explosion shattered the peaceful serenity of the Maui countryside. Unseen projectiles ripped through palm trees, mangling fronds and scattering birds from their nests. Dirt and smoke filled the sky, momentarily blocking out the sun.

The sudden impact of something weighty rammed into Kiki Brill's back, cutting off her scream. She plummeted forward onto the hard-packed earth, scraping her knees and elbows.

Heaviness smothered her, trapping her flat against the ground and knocking the breath from her lungs in a whoosh.

Panic shot through her brain in a fireworks display of red and white. She struggled against the bulky weight, clawing at the dirt, trying to breathe, to gain some leverage to get out from beneath whatever had landed on her.

Desperation labored in her lungs. The stench of fertilizer overwhelmed her senses.

"Hey, watch it!" a male voice close to her ear shouted.

Fresh panic tore a path through her mind and pumped adrenaline in her veins. She twisted and bucked, needing to free herself of the man atop her.

A momentary easing of the man's weight renewed her efforts. She kicked and pushed, managing to scramble away.

She jumped to her feet ready to bolt, but as her gaze landed on the man, her heart stalled and cemented her to the spot. *What?*

Ryan McClain, his richly made business suit covered in dirt and fertilizer, sat on his backside on the path leading to the greenhouse. Muck caked his dark hair and his turbulent, mocha-colored eyes stared at her with a mixture of panic and bewilderment.

She forced a breath in and coughed, spitting out dusty gunk that matched the floating bits in the air.

Her mind tried to make sense of what had happened. Something had exploded. Ryan McClain was sitting at her feet. Innately she knew he'd used his body to shield her, protecting her from the blast.

Fear gripped her in a tight vise. *Tutu?*

Her gaze jerked to the main house, just past the greenhouse where she'd been headed. The thatched roof and clapboard-sided structure still stood, looking undamaged.

"Tutu!" she yelled anyway, and ran for the front

door, aware of Ryan vaulting to his feet and running behind her.

Grandmother Kaapa stood on the porch, her dark eyes wide with panic, but otherwise she seemed unhurt. Even at barely five feet tall, Lana Kaapa had a commanding presence.

Lana's long, dark, gray-streaked hair was gathered into a loose bun, and a hibiscus blossom rested at her ear. Her blue-and-white floral housedress reached her ankles and revealed the ballerina-style slippers Kiki had brought her from Philadelphia.

Kiki launched herself into her grandmother's arms.

"You're okay?" Kiki gasped, panting in terror.

"Yes, dear." Tutu pulled Kiki back to inspect her. Tears gathered in her eyes. "Are you hurt?"

Kiki shook her head as relief spread through her system, but the panic and fear wouldn't release their grip. "What happened?"

Tutu shook her head, anxiety clouding her eyes. "I don't know. I was resting and I heard a loud bang. I came out to see this." She gestured with her hand toward the small grassy yard and beyond to the crops of plant life, which stretched to the cliffs that kept the Kaapa Flower farm in business.

Kiki turned to look and sucked in a sharp breath. A dark layer of grime coated everything—the swaying Tahitian ginger plants, the various colored proteas, the sunny cup of gold blossoms and all the other plants. Even the porch was dusted with gunk.

She could feel the filth on her own skin through the cotton of her T-shirt and her green board shorts. Could see it floating in the air.

Then her gaze landed on Ryan at the foot of the stairs, his expression concerned as he stared back at her. The memory of what he'd done hit her smack in the middle. He'd used his body to shield her from the explosion.

Kiki turned to her grandmother. "Call the police, please, Tutu."

Looking dazed with worry, Tutu nodded and headed back inside.

Facing Ryan, Kiki said, "Thank you." She suddenly felt self-conscious as she descended the porch steps. She could only assume she looked as filthy as he did. His navy pinstriped suit was ruined and his once-shiny black shoes would need more than just a polish. "Do you know what happened?"

His troubled brown gaze met hers. "I just got here. Saw you, headed over to talk to you, and as I closed in something went *ka-boom*."

Something? Her gaze searched for the origin of the explosion. She walked down the path toward where the company trucks were parked. "My fertilizer truck!"

Ryan joined her on the path. "It *was* your fertilizer truck. I'd say that's what we have all over us."

Slanting him a sideways glance, her lip curled upward. "You think?"

He grinned. That same drop-dead grin that he'd used on her the first time he'd come to the flower farm five months ago to try to buy her out. Only now that smile held more charm and appeal, even coated with flecks of dirt.

He'd protected her, putting his own life in jeopardy.

Her heart did a double Dutch jump. But then a thought occurred to her. She narrowed her gaze. Had he blown up her truck? Distrust wound itself around her in a choking grip.

The squeal of sirens filled the air, distracting her. Two police cars sped up the dirt drive that ran alongside the fenced-in crop of indigenous and exotic flowers, a cloud of dust billowing in their wake.

She turned on her bare heel and walked back toward to the front yard. Tutu was already waiting to greet the officers. Two men stepped out of each car.

"The explosion came from the fertilizer truck," Kiki yelled and pointed the way.

While three of the officers headed in the direction of the smoldering remains of the fertilizer truck, one man came straight to Tutu. Nikolao Abiko, Kiki's kalabash-cousin, the Hawaiian term for close as a cousin but not by blood.

Tall, handsome and very much Hawaiian, Nikolao had been around Kiki her whole life. Seeing him here in an official capacity in his navy uniform with its yellow patches didn't feel right, wasn't normal.

But nothing about this day was normal.

She swung around to tell Ryan he should go and rammed smack into him. His warm breath fanned over her cheek.

"Hey." She gestured with her hands. "Have you never heard of personal space?"

His dark eyes flashed with humor as he stepped back. "Sorry. Didn't mean to intrude inside your bubble."

She approached Tutu and Nik in the driveway with Ryan on her heels.

Surprise and recognition showed in Tutu's eyes. "Ryan McClain, I thought that was you. By the looks of it, you've been here for a while."

Ryan smiled wryly. "Yes. For a bit."

Ryan took Tutu's fragile hand. Even after years of sun and despite her own natural darker Hawaiian skin tone, the blue veins beneath her thinning skin could be seen.

He brought her hand to his mouth and placed a kiss on her knuckles. "How are you, Auntie Lana?"

Using the traditional title of Auntie for someone older than one's self showed respect in the Hawaiian culture. Kiki was impressed, even though she didn't want to be. He at least hadn't come to the island thumbing his nose at their customs.

Kiki rolled her eyes as her grandmother's smile widened.

"Gotta love a man with classy manners," Tutu

commented, her worried dark eyes showing appreciation.

Kiki would give him the manners, but his charm could only be calculated and didn't fool her for a moment. No man that suave could be sincere.

Tutu made the introduction to Nik. "Ryan McClain, this is Officer Nik Abiko."

As Ryan's gaze turned to Nik, the charm receded, and in its place was a shrewder look that matched the one in Nik's eyes. "Officer." Ryan put out his hand.

The men shook hands. "McClain. I have to ask what you are doing here," Nik said.

"Mr. McClain was just leaving," Kiki interjected. No way did she want Ryan to explain the purpose of his visit with Tutu standing there, because he undoubtedly had come back to take another run at buying their land. And Kiki had no intention of letting her heritage go.

Nik shot Kiki a hard look. "No one leaves until we know how and why the truck blew up."

Knowing there was no way around Ryan answering Nik's questions, Kiki took Lana's hand. "Let's go back inside, Tutu, and let Nik do his job."

Tutu squeezed her hand. "I know why Ryan is here, dear."

Kiki sighed. Of course Tutu knew. Why else would McClain have come back other than to try to buy the farm from them?

Nik arched an eyebrow. "Care to enlighten me?"

"I represent a developer and a group of investors who would like to purchase the land from the Kaapa family," Ryan explained, and handed Nik a business card.

"We are not selling," Kiki stated for everyone to hear, while she stared hard at Ryan, willing him to back off. She didn't want to upset Tutu any further; she'd had enough trauma for one day.

Nik slanted Kiki a glance full of censure as he took the card and stared at it for a moment before pocketing it. "So your visit here is purely business?"

"For the most part. I do hope to present Mrs. Kaapa with a new offer to buy her property, but I also hope to learn to bodysurf," Ryan said, his mocha-colored eyes full of determination.

Kiki groaned inwardly. Great. The sweet-talking charmer *was* bent on convincing her grandmother to sell. Well, Kiki wouldn't let him.

"Is that your rental parked over there?" Nik asked, drawing Ryan's attention away.

Kiki glanced at the white, or rather the once-white, Mustang convertible parked beneath a tree. She hadn't noticed it before in all the confusion.

"Yes," Ryan confirmed.

Another officer came running up. "Hey, Nik, looks like a homemade pipe bomb."

"Have you called the forensic team?"

"They're on their way," he replied, before heading back to where the other two officers were waiting.

"How long before the explosion did you arrive?" Nik asked, his voice intense.

"Just a few minutes. I'd seen Kiki walking toward the greenhouse. I'd almost caught up to her when the truck blew."

"Did you see anyone else around?"

He shook his head. "No."

"On the highway?"

Ryan's eyebrows drew together in a concerned frown. "I passed a nondescript brown sedan, but I didn't see where the car had come from or get a good look at the driver."

Nik addressed Kiki and her grandmother. "Do either of you know why someone would want to blow up your truck?"

Kiki hated to even think the thought that ran through her head much less say it, but she had to. "I had to lay off ten workers yesterday. And at three today I told everyone else to take the rest of the afternoon off."

Nik's dark eyes were grim. "That might be reason enough. I'll need a list of names and numbers of the laid-off employees. In fact, why don't you give me a list of all the employees. Maybe someone saw something before they left."

Kiki nodded, her gut clenching. She'd tried to make it clear to the employees she'd laid off that the decision had been purely business and not personal. She hadn't wanted to lay anyone off, but the farm wasn't doing as well this season.

Last week a goat had managed to get into the crop and destroy thousands of dollars worth of plants. Then the electricity in the greenhouse went on the fritz and they'd lost some very rare species of orchids.

A bright yellow Jeep screamed up the drive and halted with squealing tires and a cloud of dust.

"Uh-oh, Pa-no," Kiki remarked, using her childhood refrain as she watched her cousin jump out of his vehicle and hustle his bulky frame toward them. When he got close enough, she subtly sniffed him. Thankfully, today he was sober.

"What happened?" Pano demanded as he stopped beside Nik.

Nik explained.

Pano's dark eyes widened. "Good thing no one was hurt." Taking his grandmother's hands in his, he asked, "Tutu, are you sure you're not hurt? I came the minute I heard. Is there anything I can do?"

Lana's soft smile was full of love for her grandson. "No, dear. The police are doing what they can. I'm grateful you came, though."

Pano's gaze shifted to Ryan. "Hey, aren't you the guy who was here last spring, wanting to buy this place?"

"Yes," Ryan answered.

Pano's gaze narrowed. "Did you do this?"

That was the same question Kiki had considered. She watched Ryan closely as he shook his head, his gaze direct and honest.

"No, I didn't. But I can see how this doesn't look good for me." Ryan turned to address Nik. "I'll cooperate fully in your investigation. I have nothing to hide."

Nik nodded his thanks. "That's appreciated. I'll have more questions I'm sure."

"Why don't you ask him about the deal the neighbors have?" Pano suggested to Nik, his gaze hard on Ryan.

Kiki flitted a glance at Ryan as wariness twisted in her gut. Deal?

"The neighbors on both sides of the property want to sell, but the deal won't go through unless the investors I represent have this land, as well," Ryan explained.

Anger shot through Kiki. Had one of her neighbors done this? "The neighbors are just going to have to live with disappointment."

"When did you make this deal with the neighbors?" Nik asked.

"We've been in negotiations since last May," Ryan responded.

Kiki blinked as disbelief swept through her.

He'd been talking to their neighbors even after she'd told him they wouldn't sell?

Now Mr. Laanui's comment at the grocery store last month made sense. The old man had cornered her in the produce section. "You're standing in the way," he'd stated in English, his black eyes cold.

She'd assumed he meant she was in his way with her cart, but now she wasn't so sure. Could he have blown up her truck? Or had one of the other neighbors?

"Pano, I'm sure Ryan had nothing to do with this," Tutu stated firmly. "He is a guest on the island and would like to learn to bodysurf. Why don't you take him tomorrow?" Tutu suggested, though judging by the forceful look in her dark eyes she expected Pano to do as she asked.

For a moment, Kiki didn't think Pano would comply. But then he relented and nodded.

"Sure. You up for that?" Pano asked Ryan.

Ryan gave Pano a thumbs-up sign. Kiki's teeth clenched. The last thing she needed was Ryan and Pano buddying up, giving Ryan an opportunity to convince Pano to advocate the sale of the land. She wasn't sure where Pano stood on the issue. He'd never taken much of an interest in the business, even though he'd grown up on the farm. He'd moved out as soon as he could and now lived in a beachside apartment complex in Kihei.

A shrill ringing filled the air.

"I'll get it," said Tutu. She hurried toward the house.

At the questioning looks of the men, Kiki explained, "We have the phone set up on a loudspeaker system so we can hear it if we're in the field or the greenhouse."

"You'd definitely be able to hear that," quipped Ryan.

"Where are you staying, McClain?" Pano asked.

"The Mana Kai."

Nik nodded. "If I have any more questions for you, I'll know where to find you."

"Kiki!" Tutu called from the doorway.

"Excuse me." Kiki left the three men talking and hurried to the house, careful not to brush against the floral couch. Tutu sat in a cane-back chair at the dining table, the phone sitting on the table. There was a strange expression on Tutu's face.

"What's wrong?" Kiki asked, concern running cold in her veins.

Tutu gestured to the phone. "Your father is on the line."

Kiki picked it up. "Daddy?"

"Hi, sweetheart. There's an issue that you need to know about. An ex-con named Jeff Tolar, who was released six months ago, has vowed revenge on your grandfather for putting him away."

Distress tightened Kiki's lungs. She pulled out a chair and sat next to Tutu. Tutu wrapped her hand around Kiki's free hand.

"What did Grandfather put him away for?"

"Second-degree murder. During a convenience-store robbery, the store clerk tried to stop Tolar. He shot and killed the clerk during the ensuing struggle. Tolar claimed he'd never intended to hurt anyone.

Your grandfather gave the guy the max. But he got out early on a technicality. Earlier this week, your grandfather's office was ransacked and the only thing missing was his photo of the grandkids."

Kiki knew immediately which picture he referred to. At Christmas four years ago, all the grandkids had posed in front of the old white oak tree outside of her grandparents' home. It had been the first time in years that the six of them had all been together for the holiday. The picture had sat on her grandfather's sideboard in his judge's chambers ever since.

There'd been threats made on the family over the years, even a few attempts directly made on her grandfather's life. Most judges received them at one time or another. Whenever a threat was made, the whole family went on alert. "You'll keep Mother safe?"

"Of course. We all have protection here."

"How's Grandfather taking this?" Kiki asked, picturing in her mind the tough judge whose gruff voice and craggy face had frightened Kiki as a child.

"In stride. But he's getting on in years and is thinking about retiring."

Kiki didn't have any strong feelings one way or another about her grandfather's retirement. She'd never been close to her father's parents even though she'd grown up near them in Philadelphia. "Please give everyone my love and tell them I'll be praying for them."

"I will. But Kiki, you have to be careful, okay?"

"It's highly unlikely this Jeff Tolar guy is going to come to the island looking for me."

"The police think otherwise. Promise me if any strangers come around, you'll contact the police and me ASAP."

Kiki frowned as the events of the day played out in her head. Surely one didn't have anything to do with the other. Did it?

Her father's words replayed in her head. *An ex-con released six months ago.* About the time that Ryan had first shown up. Coincidence? Or was there something more sinister about his appearance at the Kaapa farm?

The hair at the nape of her neck shimmied with awareness. She knew before she even turned her gaze that she'd find Ryan standing in the doorway, filling the frame with his presence.

And blocking the only escape.

TWO

Turning her face away from Ryan and lowering her voice, Kiki said, "There has been a stranger here wanting to buy the farm."

"Give me his name and I'll have the FBI run a check on him," Hunter said, his voice echoing her anxiety.

As a well-respected lawyer in his own right, Hunter had connections in all areas of law enforcement. Kiki gave him the information, aware that Tutu had moved to talk quietly with Ryan.

"Also, Daddy, someone blew up the fertilizer truck today. The police said it was a homemade pipe bomb."

"Kiki, you and Lana come to Philly immediately," he demanded, his voice hard and laced with worry.

"No, Daddy," Kiki replied with a good dose of stubbornness. They'd been down this road several times over the last year. Her parents thought she was wasting her talents on a business that had never really seen great success. Kiki's mother wanted Lana to sell and move to Philadelphia to live with them. And she'd been very upset about Kiki's decision to move to Maui. Kiki didn't understand how her mother could turn her back on her heritage, a thing Kiki could never do. Not even an explosion could make her go back to Philadelphia and the life she'd had there.

"At least until all this unpleasantness is settled," he insisted.

"No," she repeated. If there was danger here on the island, she'd rather trust the Maui police to protect her and Tutu than go back to Philly and subject herself and Tutu to her father's family.

There was a moment of silence. Kiki could picture the frustrated tick in her father's hard jaw.

"I'll check on this McClain fellow and get back to you. Until then don't let him in the house," he finally said.

It's a little late for that, Kiki thought as she watched her grandmother hand Ryan a glass of water. "Hurry."

"Be very careful."

"I will." Kiki hung up and faced Ryan. He looked ridiculously handsome, despite the flecks of fertilizer clinging to his suit, and nothing like a hardened criminal. But one could never tell. "Is Nik still outside?"

Ryan nodded. "The forensic team just showed up."

"Good." Kiki moved closer to her grandmother.

"I'm sure Nik is done questioning you. You can leave now."

He blinked at her blatant attempt to get rid of him. "Actually, I'm blocked in."

Crud. Kiki tapped her foot. How long would it take her father to have a background check run on the man?

"Won't you stay for dinner?" Lana asked, always the polite hostess.

Kiki shook her head. "I'm sure Mr. McClain would like to clean up. I know I would."

Tutu laughed. "I've grown used to the smell."

Ryan smiled. "Dinner would be great, but perhaps another time."

"Tomorrow?" Tutu pressed.

"Works for me," Ryan answered. "But I really should see if I can get back to the condo and clean up."

"Yes, that's a great idea," Kiki stated, and preceded him out the door.

Ryan suppressed a grin. She really was something, this Hawaiian beauty. Her long tan legs carried her with a swift, economical stride. Everything about her was tightly contained, but the woman clearly had fire in her blood. And obviously even a bomber couldn't intimidate her.

He frowned, not liking that someone had committed such a dangerous act. Kiki and her grandmother could really have been hurt had they been closer to the truck.

Kiki flipped her dark braid over her shoulder, the thick end nearly clobbering him in the face. She'd probably hoped it would. For some reason she didn't like him.

Having a woman respond so negatively was an odd experience for him when he poured on extra charm. For as long as he could remember, females flocked to him with as little encouragement as a smile.

But not Kiki Brill.

No, from the moment she'd laid eyes on him last May she'd bristled like a porcupine caught in the glare of headlights.

Today was no different. When she scrambled away after the blast, her gold-speckled eyes had widened with a mixture of disbelief and something else that he'd been unable to identify. And then her gaze had turned cold and the lines around her lush red lips had tightened.

From the moment she'd opened her mouth, she'd made it clear he wasn't welcome, which only fueled his desire to breach her wall of resistance.

Because with enough charm and persistence, he would get his way. He would not fail. Failing wasn't something he did graciously. Or often.

He wanted to close the deal and acquire the second half of his bonus so he could move on to other projects. The delay in convincing Kiki and Lana to sell stressed Ryan's game plan. Not something he took lightly.

From his vantage point behind Kiki, he noted the

regal manner with which she walked down the porch, so straight and tall, as if ready to conquer the world, and it called to something deep in Ryan.

Pano and Nik stopped talking as Kiki and Ryan approached.

Nik's dark, assessing gaze reminded Ryan of his brother Brody, also a law enforcement man. Ryan supposed it was a trick of the trade, watching and analyzing every person. Brody was good at the law thing. Nik probably was, too.

But Ryan wasn't sure what to make of Pano, who wore a T-shirt with a restaurant logo emblazoned across the back and red board shorts that fell just above his knees. He looked very much like the stereotypical Polynesian man.

Pano was huge in height and mass, with broad features and jet-black eyes and hair. Kiki's curvy statuesque build, crowned by her shiny black-brown hair, gold-specked brown eyes and symmetrical features made it seem as if they weren't from the same gene pool.

And looking at Lana Kaapa, who had joined them outside, he could see that she had different features than either of her grandchildren. Lana's rounded face, kind brown eyes and diminutive stature made Ryan wonder about the two cousins' parents.

Granted, not all relatives resembled each other. Ryan and his sister, Megan, favored their mother's side of the family, except for Ryan's dark eyes. Only his sister, out of the four siblings, had been blessed with the Kelley blues. Ryan's older brothers, Brody and Patrick, both resembled their father in looks, but also their grandfather Connor McClain.

"Officer, do you need anything else from me?" Ryan asked.

"No, you're good to go. Just don't leave the island," Nik responded.

Pano tipped his chin in Ryan's direction. "Tomorrow I can take you out to Makena Beach. Good surfing there."

"Makena Beach is fine." Ryan turned to Lana. "I'm sorry for the trouble you've had today. If there is anything I can do, let me know."

She patted his arm. "We'll see you for dinner tomorrow."

He met Kiki's smoldering gaze. Whether she liked it or not, Ryan was going to make this sale go through.

One way or another.

Anger simmered low in Kiki's gut as she watched Ryan drive his rented Mustang out of sight. He seemed to have her Tutu wrapped around his little finger. He wouldn't be so successful with Kiki.

Why hadn't her father called back? It would ease her mind if she could confirm Ryan's true identity. Then all she'd have to worry about was his smooth-talking sales pitch and not whether he was going to try to hurt her to get back at her grandfather.

Ha! As if her grandfather would even bat an eye if anything were to happen to Kiki or her mother. The judge hadn't been coy in making his feelings known over the years. The Brills had never forgiven or forgotten that their son Hunter had turned his back on the debutante they'd picked out for him.

Even to this day, Sophia Brill, Hunter's mother, kept tabs on the woman who should have been her daughter-in-law. Kiki didn't know how her mother put up with the Brill family.

Shaking off the unanswerable question, Kiki turned to Nik. "My father will be calling you about…something else." She didn't want to reveal anything more in front of Ryan.

Interest gleamed in Nik's gaze. "I'll look forward to hearing from him."

Glad he didn't press, she asked, "You'll let us know if you find out who did this?"

He nodded. "Yes, as soon as I know, I'll let you know."

"Good." She surveyed the mess. Not much to be done other than pick up the metal and sweep the paths and porch. The fertilizer wasn't going to hurt anything.

The phone rang. Kiki sprinted back inside.

"Hello?"

"It's me." Hunter said. "This McClain fellow is who he says."

Relief spread through her. At least Ryan wouldn't be trying to kill her. "Thanks, Daddy."

"Are you sure you won't come home?"

Kiki closed her eyes. She missed her mother and father, but not the stress of not being good enough for the rest of the Brills. "Why don't you and Mom come here?"

"You know we can't. The judge needs me here."

"Of course." Kiki tried not to be bitter, but for her whole life, everything always revolved around the judge and what he needed. "Tell Mom I love her."

"I will, dear. I'm also going to fax a photo of Tolar to the local police there and will send one to your e-mail. Promise me you'll be careful."

"Of course. Don't worry, nothing is going to happen to me."

"I love you, Kiki." Hunter's voice softened.

Kiki smiled. "I love you, too, Daddy."

After they hung up, Kiki went to the front window of the house. Her gaze landed briefly on her island family as they still talked in the front yard, then her gaze moved on to where the forensic people were doing whatever they did at a crime scene.

A crime scene. Here on the farm.

The idea was so surreal, yet someone had blown up the fertilizer truck. Why? What could anyone possibly gain by doing such a thing?

She shook her head at the futileness of the question. Nik would uncover the truth. She'd trust him to do that.

She focused her gaze on the lush green fields of flowers—the striking bird-of-paradise, the rich reds of the ruellias and the pink ginger which she loved so much—that extended all the way to the rugged cliffs that dropped to a beautiful cove below. The Pacific Ocean's soothing song could be heard crashing against the shore. A slight trade wind sent the colorful blossoms dancing in a bright display of pinks, reds and whites. A sight that never failed to bring a smile to Kiki's heart.

The years of hard work and love that each flower represented filled Kiki with a fierce determination. This farm was her heritage, her birthright, and she would do anything to protect it, no matter how much money was offered. She couldn't allow anyone to stand in her way.

Especially, not Ryan McClain.

The next morning, Ryan sat in a tall metal chair on the small lanai of his rented condo, contemplating his view of Keawakapu's sandy beach. The churning surf beyond was breathtaking in the morning light. The happy sounds of children already enjoying the day drifted on the slight trade winds that didn't cool the already humid temperatures.

Closer in, the lush grassy lawn which stretched from the back entry of the building to meet the sandy beach was filling with people claiming their lawn chairs with towels and other fun-in-the sun paraphernalia. The oval-shaped pool with its beautiful rock waterfall looked inviting as people who preferred the less harsh water of the pool to the ocean began splashing around.

Last night before turning in for the night, Ryan had taken a swim in the pool and found the non-chlorinated, nonsalty water very refreshing. He could get used to this lifestyle. Back home in Boston, the leaves would be turning and the air temperature falling.

He didn't miss the cold. But since he had no intention of staying in Hawaii until it was summer again in Boston, he'd just as soon take advantage of the warmth of the tropical island now.

A knock at the condo door brought him to his water-sandal-clad feet. He'd dressed in board shorts and a body-hugging shirt called a rashguard to keep both the sun and the rough sand from doing damage to his very underexposed skin. He tugged at the high collar as he approached the door.

Expecting to see Pano, he was pleasantly surprised to open the door and find Kiki on his doorstep, looking very lovely in her bright pink shorts, matching tank top and flip-flops with little white daisys attached to the straps. Once again her dark hair was gathered in a braid falling over one shoulder.

He grinned. "Hi. This is unexpected." But nice.

She gave him a stiff smile. "Pano called and asked if I'd bring you out. He had to work on the other side of the island early this morning and will meet us there."

"Great." Leaving the door open, he went to gather his belongings, including a small cooler filled with water bottles and snacks he'd bought at the grocery store last night.

"You're prepared," Kiki said as he joined her in the hallway.

He shrugged. "Always. Growing up, I never knew what my brothers were going to throw at me, so being prepared became a habit."

They rode the elevator in silence, but Ryan couldn't help but notice in the mirrored reflection of the walls how long and shapely Kiki's legs were, or how defined the muscles in her arms were. She not only had a strong personality, but she was physically fit. He liked that about her.

Once outside the building, Kiki led him to a red Volkswagen Rabbit with the top down. Kiki climbed behind the wheel and put on a pair of sunglasses. Putting the cooler on the backseat next to another small cooler, Ryan climbed into the passenger seat. "You came prepared, as well."

One side of her mouth quirked up. "Always."

Ryan laughed and settled back to enjoy the ride. Kiki maneuvered the car through the Saturday-morning traffic of Kihei and soon they were buzzing along the Piilani Highway and past neighborhoods filled with older homes, past newer developments and stretches of undeveloped parcels of land dotted with swaying palms and other tropical flora. They seemed to be heading away from the coast and up a small incline.

"What does Pano do that he'd have to work so early?"

"He works for the state on a construction crew for the roads. Everyone complains when the work is done during high-traffic times."

"Ah. Makes sense."

The terrain shifted as they headed back toward the coast. More condominium complexes with manicured lawns dotted one side of the road while the other side had big, fancy hotels with pristine landscaping. Ryan caught brief glimpses of the ocean beyond. Jogging paths and bicycle lanes were full of people.

The condos eventually gave way to a sprawling golf course and an upscale-looking shopping center. A place he would have to visit before returning home.

Then the road curved and narrowed to a more residential area. They passed makeshift roadside restaurants and a woman sitting under an umbrella with a large display of jewelry for sale.

Ryan's gaze took in the rooflines of the houses along the ocean side of the road behind tall brick walls and formidable hedges. "These are some big homes."

"Most are second homes for mainlanders with

money to burn," she said with just the slightest trace
of bitterness.

Did most islanders feel as though they'd been in-
vaded by the wealthy mainlanders?

"You know, if you sell the land, you and Tutu
could afford a house like one of these, right on the
beach," he stated, not sure Kiki would be the type to
want to live in such an opulent place. She seemed
quite content in the little run-down home of her an-
cestors.

"What will it hurt for you and your grandmother
to at least see the newest offer?" And accept it, he
hoped.

Her shoulders tensed. "Nothing, I guess. But don't
get your hopes up."

"Why is the farm so important to you?"

She glanced at him, her eyes imploring him to
understand. "It's home for me."

"I thought you grew up in Pennsylvania?"

"I did. But the mainland has never *felt* like home."

"There are more…comfortable places to live on
the island."

The dark sunglasses obscured her eyes, but the
quirk of her mouth showed her disdain. "You don't
get it. You're a mainlander. The islands are more than
just pretty beaches."

"But business is business whether in Boston,
Philadelphia or Hawaii. Progress can't be stopped.
And quality of life has to be a factor in the decision
process."

She blew out a frustrated breath. "I can turn the farm around. I just need time."

"Time isn't your friend here, Kiki. The investors are getting anxious. If they can't get what they want here, they'll move on and the offer will be rescinded."

Her chin jutted out in a stubborn gesture that reminded him of his sister when she'd set her mind to something. "Then that's just too bad."

There was no point in arguing with her at this point. Lana Kaapa would be the deciding factor. He'd have to wait until she looked at the proposal before he really got down to the business of convincing the women of Kaapa Flower Farm to sell.

And, yes, he would convince them to sell. He was known for closing the deal—that was why Horatio Lewis had hired him. Ryan would do what it took to make the sale go through; his reputation was on the line.

"Will you at least look at the offer?"

For a moment he didn't think she'd answer. Finally she said, "Yes."

"Thank you."

Her only response was a tightening of her lips. Ryan decided not to push right now. He had to gain her trust before he pressed her to give in to his way of thinking.

The road narrowed even more and then Kiki turned on to a dirt road. The convertible bounced along until Ryan thought his teeth would rattle out of his mouth. Kiki brought the car to a halt next to Pano's yellow Jeep. After the cloud of dust cleared,

Ryan noted there were several he-man type vehicles parked in the makeshift parking lot.

He and Kiki made their way through tall grass and swaying palms to a wide expanse of white sandy beach and blue-green waves. Overhead, white puffy clouds formed interesting shapes in the stunning blue sky.

Kiki kicked off her shoes and left them where they landed, heading toward a group of six people clustered on the beach. Ryan left his sandals on, the soft sand sinking with each step as he followed Kiki.

"Hey, cousin, thanks for picking up the Haole," Pano called as they approached. He wore a short-sleeved, knee-length body-hugging yellow wet suit. It made a statement, like his Jeep.

Two of the men and one of the women wore the same sort of neoprene gear, only in more subdued black or blue. Ryan shook hands with Pano, his girl-friend, Carol, and the others as Pano introduced his coworkers and their girlfriends.

Ryan was careful to keep his eye contact, which could be mistaken as a sign of aggression, to a mini-mum so as not to breach the cultural barrier. He didn't want any trouble with these men or the women, who giggled as they were introduced.

Pano picked up a black wet suit from a pile of towels resting on a boulder. "Here." He held it out to Ryan. "You'll need to wear this."

"Okay." Ryan set his belongings down and took

the suit. Conscious of all eyes watching him, he stepped into the clinging, stiff material.

Pano clapped him on the back as some of the others, ready to surf, headed to the water. "Come on, *haumana*. Let's rock and roll."

"I'm ready. What's *haumana*?" He hoped it didn't mean shark bait.

Pano grinned, his white, even teeth gleaming in the warm sunlight. "Student."

Ryan saluted Kiki before she turned away to talk with the two women who'd not gone in the water. Ryan jogged down to the water's edge where the surf turned over with a tremendous amount of force.

He hoped he didn't drown, or worse yet, make a fool of himself in front of Kiki. She already had held him in enough disdain without adding some embarrassing mishap to his credit.

He was going to drown.

It was all Kiki could do not to run into the water and grab Ryan by the back of his wet suit and drag his sorry hide out of the water.

Why hadn't he said he wasn't a strong swimmer?

She winced as the surf rolled him over and pounded him into the sand. He gamely wobbled back to his feet, listened intently to Pano's instructions and headed back out.

The man really had a determined spirit about him

that Kiki admired. And feared. If he put this much energy and tenacity into trying to convince her and Tutu to sell, Kiki wasn't sure he wouldn't wear her down.

But she had to stay strong. Her future depended on it.

On the blanket next to Kiki, Ginger Tao yelled as she posed her bikini-clad body to advantage, "Good job, Ryan. Keep at it, you'll get it."

Kiki shot Ginger a sidelong glance and resisted the urge to clamp a hand over Ginger's mouth to stop her encouragement. Ryan needed to get out of the water before he got hurt, not be egged on to keep beating himself up in the waves.

Ginger shielded her eyes with a hand over her brow. "He's single, right?"

"I don't know," Kiki answered, willing the spurt of…of something…that she didn't want to feel to die a quick death.

"I hope he is," remarked Carol Gagtan as she lifted her thick brown hair off her neck.

Kiki snorted. "What about Pano?"

Carol shrugged, clearly not as committed to Kiki's cousin as Pano thought. "Do either of you have a scrunchie?"

"In my car," Kiki said, and rose. "I'll go grab one for you."

It beat watching Ryan torture himself in the surf. She personally had never understood the allure of bodysurfing. Board surfing, yeah. It was a rush. That she liked. "Be back in a second."

When she reached her car, she went to the passenger side to open the glove box where she kept extra hair bands. A white envelope lay on the driver's seat. What was this?

There was no writing on the outside. She flipped the envelope over. It hadn't been sealed. Curious, she lifted the flap. A folded sheet of paper was inside. Using her fingernails, she pulled the paper out and unfolded it.

She blinked in surprise. In letters cut from what looked like a newspaper or magazine was a message.

You sell farm or you regret.

Kiki sucked in a sharp breath and jerked her gaze up to scan the parking area. There were no new cars parked in the lot. No one visibly lurked around.

Someone must have followed her here and waited until she'd gone to the beach to leave the note. Unless…unless Ryan left the envelope on the seat when he got out and was going to pretend the threat was from someone else.

She dismissed the idea. That didn't feel right. He might want her to sell the farm but he wasn't a criminal. She couldn't see him stooping so low now. He seemed more straightforward and honest.

Then who?

The same person who blew up the truck?

Angry at the note, the note writer and herself for being spooked, she grabbed a scrunchie out of the glove box, shoved the note among the other hair bands and slammed the compartment closed.

She'd figure out what to do about the note later. Right now she needed to go home and make sure nothing bad happened.

Apprehension scraped along her nerves. She shivered even as the sun beat down on her shoulders with enough heat to redden her brown skin.

Was Tutu in danger?

THREE

Ryan come up for air after being smashed into the ground for the umpteenth time in the last hour and noticed a certain tall beauty missing. He immediately headed for dry land and refused to look at the reason for his concern…no, make that curiosity.

He accepted the towel Ginger held out with a smile. "Thanks. Where's Kiki?"

"She went to get me a scrunchie," replied Carol, her dark eyes assessing him as she gathered her thick hair in her hand and lifted the mass up off her shoulders, exposing the long brown-skinned column of her throat in a practiced move.

"She's not true Hawaiian, you know," Ginger remarked.

Ryan's smile tightened in annoyance. He didn't like the way the woman made Kiki's mixed heritage sound second-rate. "Beats not being Hawaiian at all."

"You like Kiki?" Carol asked, her gaze speculative.

Hmm. Good question.

He'd certainly enjoyed verbally sparring with her since he'd first contacted her for his client last spring. He appreciated her loyalty and dedication to her grandmother and the family business that produced some beautiful product. "Sure."

He liked her. To his surprise, a lot. But his feelings for Kiki had nothing to do with his purpose for being on Maui.

The smirk on Carol's face made the hair on the back of his neck rise. He could *feel* Kiki behind him.

Prepared for some smart remark, he put his most lethally charming smile in place and turned around, but one look at Kiki's tense face killed the smile.

She was upset and he instinctively doubted her distress had anything to do with overhearing Carol's question or his answer.

He stepped closer and took her hands. "What's wrong?"

For a moment indecision crossed her face, then she pulled her hands away from him. "Nothing."

Her denial didn't ring true. "Something."

She slipped a red fabric elastic band from around her wrist and handed it to Carol. To Ryan she said, "Pano can return you to your condo."

Taken aback, he frowned. "You're leaving?" He searched her face. What was she thinking now?

She turned away to gather her things.

No way was he letting this opportunity to build trust between them slip through his hands. "I'm coming with you."

Keeping her back to him she said, "No need."

But he did need to. He needed to keep the lines of communication open between them. He wanted to.

"Yes, there is. I'm done for the day," he replied, unzipping the wet suit, which clung to him like a second skin and peeled the thing off.

"See you two later. I'm going to go see if the boys are ready for lunch," Ginger said, and ran off toward the water.

With a sly smile, Carol followed Ginger, leaving Ryan alone with a quiet Kiki.

"I'm afraid I'll soak your car seat," he said.

Kiki shrugged distractedly. "No big deal. You sure you want to leave?"

He gathered his belongings together. "Yes."

She sighed. "All right, then. Hop to it."

Kiki led the way back through the grass and trees to the parking lot in silence. Ryan folded his towel in half and laid it on the seat to help absorb some of the water from his wet shorts, the lack of conversation continuing.

They drove for several minutes in silence. Along the side of the road a family of mongooses foraged for food along a hedge. Kiki and Ryan passed the woman with the jewelry stand. Ryan made a note to himself to stop there some time to pick up something pretty for his mother and sister. He slanted a glance Kiki's way.

She didn't wear jewelry. Her ears didn't have the piercings in the lobes and he hadn't yet seen her slender neck adorned with a necklace. Though he wasn't surprised that her graceful hands, with their blunt nails, didn't sport any rings, since she used her hands so much working with the plants she cultivated.

Studying her profile, the tapered nose, the high cheekbones and the concentration on her face made him wonder what was going on in Kiki's mind? The worry lines around her mouth and eyes didn't sit well with him. What had her so tied in knots? Something more than a pipe bomb?

He wanted to ease her tension and break through the barrier that kept her from agreeing to sell the parcel of land. Now might be a prime moment. Ryan asked, "Would you like to stop for lunch? I'm buying."

Her hands gripped the steering wheel so tight color drained from her knuckles. "I need to go home," Kiki stated.

He laid a hand on her arm. The warm supple skin branded his palm. "Tell me what has upset you."

"How do you know I'm upset?"

"I can just tell."

She took a deep breath and seemed to be debating with herself before she flipped on the blinker and brought the car to a halt on the side of the narrow dirt shoulder. Reaching past him, she opened the glove compartment and pulled out a white envelope. "This is why."

He slipped the folded sheet of paper out and read

the words. Shock and anger spiked in his veins. "Where did it come from?"

"When I came back to the car to get Carol a hair tie, I found the envelope with the letter inside on the seat."

Someone had been in the makeshift parking lot while they were at the beach. Concern for Kiki's welfare arced through him and overshadowed his own agenda. "You have to take this to the police."

"Right." She pulled back onto the road. "What are *they* going to do? It's just a stupid note."

That freaked her out.

"After what happened yesterday? Are you kidding me? This is a threat. Any threat should be taken seriously."

He refolded the note and tucked it back into the envelope, wishing he could as easily put away the roaring trepidation kicking its heels in his blood.

Someone wanted the flower farm sold badly enough to threaten the Kaapas.

Ryan's client, Horatio? The syntax of the note was off, though. And certainly not something Ryan pictured Horatio Lewis, the owner of the largest land development company in the nation, doing. Though there had been rumors over the past year that Horatio's business practices bordered on unethical. But on the previous deals Ryan had worked on with Horatio, Ryan hadn't seen any hint of underhanded dealings. No, the note was too…unsophisticated to have originated with Horatio. Wasn't it? "Do you think one of your neighbors could have left the note?"

"The thought occurred to me. But I can't see any of them trekking all the way here to leave a note on my car seat."

"They have something to gain if you sell the land, however."

"True." She blew out an agitated breath. "I have to check on Tutu. If something happened to her, I...I don't know what I'd do."

He held open his cell phone. "Call."

She reached for the phone, but Ryan returned her attention to the road with a tilt of his head. With another sigh, she rattled off the number and Ryan dialed. She took the phone from him while keeping one hand on the steering wheel.

After a moment, she handed it back, her eyes bleak. "No answer."

"Then let's go straight to the farm," Ryan said.

"I'll drop you off first."

"No." He wasn't about to let her walk into some unknown situation by herself. He prayed that his worry was unfounded, but just in case...he was sticking close to Kiki. "I'd like to check on your grandmother, also."

She shot him a quick glance. "Why?"

"Because I like her. And I certainly don't want anything bad to happen to her. Or you."

Her lips pursed together and she didn't comment again as she sped down the Piilani Highway into the countryside away from town. She turned the car onto the long dirt drive running alongside the fields and leading up to the ramshackle traditional-style Hawaiian house.

The rows and rows of flowering blossoms stretched toward the sun without any signs of uninvited guests. Nor were there signs of life near the greenhouse, the big huge metal building off to the left or the tiny shed barely visible beyond that.

All was quiet and still. Almost too still.

Kiki stopped the car in a spray of gravel and jumped out before the engine had even stopped rotating. Ryan quickly followed her up the porch steps. He slipped his sandals off, leaving them beside Kiki's flip-flops and entered the house.

"Tutu?" Kiki called, her voice a little high. She disappeared down the hall, only to reappear a moment later, her eyes wide and panicky. "She's not here."

Kiki looked as if she was about to hyperventilate. Ryan grasped her by the elbow and made her sit on the faded upholstered couch. "Could she be out shopping? Buying groceries?"

"I suppose." She rose and headed toward the door.

Ryan hurried after her, but he at least paused long enough to slip his sandals back on before vaulting down the porch steps to catch up with her. She halted as they rounded the corner of the house. "Her car is gone."

Relief eased through Ryan. "There you go. She's out shopping, doing errands or whatever else, so there's no reason to worry." He hoped.

"But I told her I'd get groceries after I got back from the beach. She's seventy years old, Ryan. Tutu shouldn't be out driving around."

Ryan's mouth twitched with a smile. The lady wanted to be in control and sure didn't like it when she wasn't. "Your grandmother is a vital, energetic woman who's more than capable of doing as she pleases. At her age, she's earned the right to go shopping by herself."

Kiki frowned at him. "Of course. I know that. It's just…"

"The note." The threat. The explosion yesterday. Anger burst anew in his gut.

"Yeah. The note. I'm sure it doesn't mean anything and I'm being ridiculous. It just unnerved me."

"Which I would imagine was the sender's intent. But the pipe bomb yesterday wasn't meant only to scare, it destroyed your truck. I'm telling you, call the police."

She waved his suggestion away. "Later."

"Waiting is not a good idea."

That stubborn, you're-not-going-to-tell-me-what-to-do look came into her eyes. He could argue with her until he was blue in the face and he wouldn't get anywhere. So he took a different tactic.

He grabbed her hand. "My father was a cop. One of my brothers is a sheriff. I've heard enough stories to know waiting is never a good thing when it comes to threats of any kind. Yeah, it may be nothing but it might be something and wouldn't you rather be proven right than wrong?"

Her gaze narrowed but the worry there didn't lessen. "Fine. I'll go call Nik."

"Good idea. Nik seemed competent."

Ryan released her hand and she went inside.

Taking a seat on the porch steps, Ryan blew out the tension and focused his gaze on the tropical vista spread out before him. No wonder someone had decided this piece of property would be the perfect spot for a resort.

The rolling landscape, full of colorful foliage extending toward the rugged cliffs, was a glorious contrast above the churning, white-capped waves of the Pacific Ocean. The darker hues of the water blended with the brighter blue sky at the horizon line. A truly captivating scene.

He shifted his attention to the flower farm's rows of exotic plants. He had no doubt that even when the beautiful array of red, yellow, white and pink of the cultivated flowers were gone, the view would still be breathtaking.

He could envision a lush, manicured lawn in place of the crops and a huge white gazebo for weddings.

Possibly even a small stage for miniconcerts. The place would be a gold mine in the tropics. A gold mine that would fill his own bank account.

"Nik's on his way," Kiki stated as she joined him on the stairs.

"Great." Ryan shifted his gaze to meet hers. "This would be a wonderful place for a high-end resort set up for weddings and events where people want more privacy than can be found at the other resorts right on the beach."

She frowned and turned her gaze toward the ocean. "There are other places on the island that would work. Places that aren't *currently occupied* and aren't important to me."

A cramp of remorse gripped him but he suppressed it. This was the land his client wanted. He purposefully ignored her last statement. "Really? Hmph. I didn't find any other suitable properties when I researched the island."

A flash of annoyance crossed her face. "That's because you don't know where to look."

"So where are these other places?"

"I'll show you after church tomorrow."

Was she suggesting they spend more time together? Unaccountably pleased by the notion, he teased, "Does that mean you're inviting me to church?"

She met his gaze dead on and straightened her spine. "Yes. I guess I am."

He blinked. Pleasure, followed closely by a

twinge of guilt, chased down his spine. He'd just imagined her beloved flower farm being replaced with a mega resort. How would this personal step affect his deal? Hmm. He wasn't sure he wanted to analyze that. "I would love to join you for church."

"Really? So you're a churchgoer?"

"Every Sunday, growing up. Faith is very important to my family." And to him. Though there were times he wished he understood God better.

"Good." Her mouth twisted wryly. "It's not your traditional church."

His eyebrows rose. "What does that mean? You don't offer sacrifices or burned offerings, do you?"

She laughed, the very appealing sound tingled in his chest.

"*No*, of course not," she said. "It's a Christian church, but with some Hawaiian traditions incorporated into the service."

"That sounds interesting." He held her gaze, liking how open she was at the moment.

As if she sensed his appreciation, she looked away, following the same visual path he had wandered moments ago. Though he doubted she was envisioning a five-star hotel.

"I hate this waiting. Where could Tutu be?"

The anxiousness in her pretty eyes troubled him. He wished he could lift the burden of fear off her slender shoulders. Her very personal and nonbusiness invitation to church gave him an idea. Taking a chance that she'd not rebuff him for invading her bubble, he slipped his arm around her waist, drawing her close, liking how perfectly they fit together. "Would you like to pray?"

"Oh, yes," she replied, her expression grateful and heart-wrenching. She bowed her head slightly and closed her eyes.

Writing off this very intimate action on his part as only human decency, Ryan bowed his head but kept his gaze alert for any sudden threats.

"Father God, we humbly ask for your protection over Tutu. Bring her home safely. I…"

A tear fell and landed on the dirt-covered stair by her feet. Ryan couldn't stand to see her cry and hugged her closer, aching for her and wishing he could make her fear and worry evaporate. He added his own silent prayer, *Please, God, give this woman peace and comfort and don't let anything bad happen.*

Where *was* Tutu?

Kiki shook her head and wiped at her eyes as she pulled away. "Sorry."

"No need to be. Not with me."

She smiled slightly and caught his gaze. Light flicked in the depths of her gold-flecked eyes. He wanted to reach toward the glow, to rejoice within the heat of her stare. The moment stretched as some indescribable emotion welled in his chest, constricting his breathing.

"Are you hungry?" she murmured, her voice barely above a whisper.

"Starved," he replied as his gaze dropped to her lips. What would she do if he kissed her?

She scrambled to her feet as if she'd read his thought. "Come in. I'll fix something."

Ryan shook his head to clear his thoughts, glad she'd broken the moment. Kiss her? No way was he going down some romantic road just because he'd lost his mind for a few seconds.

Pure insanity.

He was here for a reason that had nothing to do with forming an emotional relationship with Kiki. He really had to get a grip and keep focused. To remind himself of his purpose, he looked back over his shoulder at the view.

The land, vibrant and energizing in all its natural beauty from the densely tree-covered hillside, the acres of terrain with so much potential, all the way to the cliffs where the reverberation of the churning surf crashing on the rocks and sand below made a calming background sound.

Definitely worth the money Horatio was offering. The money Ryan would make if the sale went through. The money that would bring him that much closer to financial success. Then he could plan his future.

But first he had to protect his investor's interest.

FOUR

Ryan slipped out of his sandals again and stepped inside. Looking around, he reacquainted himself with the small house. Faded cloth drapes, a fabric couch that showed wear, scarred tables and lamps that looked ancient.

Considering that Mr. Kaapa's great-great-grandparents were the first to live in the house and work the farm, it was no wonder that age had taken its toll on the furnishings. No money had been spent on remodeling or updating.

Could it be that the farm always struggled or were the Kaapas tradition hounds who didn't want to replace what they'd always known?

The only visible item that brought the home into the twenty-first century was the open laptop sitting on the kitchen table. Strewn on the table beside the computer were spreadsheets and graphs. Obviously, Kiki was putting her degree in finance to work.

Kiki was in the kitchen. She pulled out sandwich

fixings from the refrigerator. "Sometimes when I'm nervous, I eat," she explained.

Having already noted how fit she was, Ryan guessed she didn't get nervous often. "Can I help?" Ryan asked as he watched her quick, efficient movements.

"Plates and cups are in the cupboard and cold lemonade in the fridge."

Soon their lunch of ham and Swiss cheese sandwiches was on plates. Kiki set a bag of chips down and then cleared away her work so they could sit across from each other at the kitchen table.

"You said one of your brothers is a cop? How many brothers do you have?"

"Two brothers, both older, and one sister."

"Is your sister younger than you?"

Ryan grinned. "No, older."

Kiki grinned back. "You're the baby?"

He rolled his eyes. "Yes."

"I've heard that birth order has a lot to do with how we turn out as adults."

Ryan lifted his eyebrow. "And?"

Kiki recalled what she'd learned in her psychology classes. "The youngest is usually charming, persuasive and likes to get his way."

"You have me pegged."

"I know," she gloated.

He sat forward. "And only children usually are perfectionists, cautious and conservative. Though some psychologist would also say spoiled is an apt adjective for an only child."

A flush of outrage heated Kiki's cheeks, but she really had no right to get mad. She'd started this. Taking a deep calming breath, she asked, "So tell me about your siblings. Since I've never had any, I'd like to know what it's like from your perspective."

"It's great and chaotic and at times really annoying, but I can't imagine my life without them. We have each other's back all the time. My two brothers are both married. Patrick, the oldest, is a professor at the University of Florida and his wife, Anne, is studying to be a teacher. Brody is the sheriff in Havensport on Nantucket. He and his wife, Kate, have a little baby boy, Joseph. My sister, Meg, lives in New York. She works in an art gallery."

"She's not married?"

He shook his head, his eyes turning troubled. "No. Meg has high-functioning OCD. She's a great girl, but she doesn't let many people get close."

"That must be hard," Kiki commented.

The front door opened and Tutu came in carrying several full shopping bags. Relief cascaded over Kiki in waves, making her feel slightly light-headed. Tutu was safe and unharmed.

Ryan quickly left the table to relieve Tutu of her burdens. Kiki appreciated Ryan's thoughtfulness. Coming in right behind Tutu was Nik, his hands laden with more bags.

"Ryan," Tutu exclaimed. "How nice to see you again. And look who drove in behind me. Ryan, you remember Nik. Nik, you remember our mainland friend, Ryan McClain."

The two men eyed each other for a moment. Then Ryan grinned, but Kiki noticed the smile didn't reach his eyes.

"Hey. I'd offer to shake hands, but we're both loaded down," he stated, and turned to take the parcels he held to the counter.

"No problem," Nik replied, and followed him into the kitchen.

The two men stood side by side as they unloaded the groceries. Kiki hadn't noticed the first time the two men were together how different in stature they were. Obviously she'd been too freaked by the fertilizer truck exploding.

But now, next to Ryan, Nik's mammoth shoulders and Polynesian good looks didn't seem nearly as compelling as they had when Kiki was a teen. She'd always thought Nik was the perfect male specimen until he'd betrayed their friendship her sixteenth summer when he'd sided with his then girlfriend who hadn't wanted the half-Haole girl hanging with them. Kiki had gotten over the hurt and had come to terms with Nik. But she'd never viewed him the same.

Nik was still good-looking and she appreciated the familiarity of his presence, but she preferred

Ryan's lean and sculpted frame, refined cheekbones and straight, well-proportioned nose.

For a mainlander he was dream. But sadly not her dream. She wouldn't give her heart to a mainlander ever again.

"Why did you call Nik?" Tutu whispered, her brown eyes worried. "Did something else blow up?"

Kiki showed her the note. Tutu's eyes grew wide. "Where did this come from?"

"Someone left it in my car this morning at the beach."

Nik approached and held out his hand. "May I?"

Kiki let him take the slip of paper, his fingers barely gripping the corner. She became aware that Ryan had come to stand beside her, so close that their shoulders touched. For some odd reason, his show of support sent a ribbon of warmth and pleasure curling through her system.

Nik glanced up. His black eyes seemed to darken as they narrowed slightly. Kiki wasn't sure if it was from the content of the note or from the protective stance that Ryan had taken. If the latter, she'd rather not know.

"You all have touched this, I take it," Nik said.

Ryan and Kiki nodded. Nik's mouth pressed into a disapproving line. "If you get any more, don't touch it. I doubt I'll get prints off this one."

"Do you think it's serious?" Tutu asked. "Is this connected to the explosion?"

Nik lifted one massive shoulder. "Could be. You should always take threats seriously, in any case."

Kiki glanced at Ryan to see if he'd gloat over being right that she should call the police, but his mocha-colored eyes were troubled as he met her gaze.

"What should the ladies do, Officer?" Ryan asked.

Nik sighed. "Make sure you report anything else suspicious or out of the ordinary. I'll tell the boys to keep their eyes and ears open. We're still waiting on results of the lab work on yesterday's pipe bomb, but I doubt we'll get anything useful."

"Actually, after I had a chance to think about it, there have been some odd things happening lately," Kiki stated. She told the men about the goat, the greenhouse electricity and what the neighbor had said to her in the grocery store.

"I'll talk with Uncle Laanui. In the meantime, you two be careful," Nik said to Kiki and Tutu, then he turned his attention to Ryan. "Are you staying here, now?"

Though the question didn't seem out of line, a tone of disapproval edged Nik's voice. Was he jealous? Kiki may have had a crush on him as a teen but he'd never treated her as anything other than a sister.

Ryan's mouth quirked as if he, too, had heard the suggestion of possessiveness in Nik's voice. "No."

Nik returned his focus to Kiki. "I'll take this."

"Fine," she replied, and tried not to let his serious

tone stir up any additional fear. She was sure that the letter was only meant to scare her.

No one would really do anything to actually hurt her or Tutu.

But she couldn't stop the sense of dread sneaking up her spine to sink its vicious fangs into her mind. She shivered.

Ryan's arm settled around her shoulders, like a protective covering. And while she appreciated his kindness, she knew only God could offer any real protection.

Protection she prayed they wouldn't need.

"Hey, Officer, could you give me a lift into Kihei?" Ryan asked. He didn't want Kiki to have to take him into town when he knew she'd be worried about leaving her grandmother alone.

"Yeah, no prob," Nik replied. He tucked the letter into the pocket of his uniform shirt. "I think you should have Pano come and stay here for a while," Nik said to Tutu.

"Do you really think that's necessary?" Kiki asked, her expression showing her dislike of the idea.

"Yes, I do," Nik responded. "Auntie Lana, I'll feel better if you'd have Pano come stay."

Tutu nodded, her eyes filled with worry. "I'll ask him."

"You might also think about installing a security system," Nik said.

Ryan thought that was a brilliant idea, but from the irritated expression on Kiki's pretty face she didn't agree. Perhaps they couldn't afford one?

"I'll look into it," Kiki replied, her tone less than thrilled.

"Let's go then, Haole," Nik said as he headed out the door. He stopped on the porch to slip his shoes back on before walking to his rig.

Tutu stopped Ryan. "You're still coming to dinner tonight?"

Ryan sought Kiki's gaze. Her expression remained neutral. "I'd love to," he replied. "I'll see you then."

Ryan closed the house door behind him, slipped on his shoes and walked to where Nik sat in his big, brown Bronco. Slipping into the passenger seat, Ryan said, "Thanks for the lift. I appreciate it."

Nik nodded and started the engine. As he drove the vehicle down the dirt drive, he asked, "So what do you *really* want with the Kaapa farm?"

"I told you, I represent some investors who'd like to buy the land. They want to build a five-star resort here."

Nik snorted. "Just what the island needs. Another resort."

"Tourism brings money," Ryan commented.

"True. But it also puts a strain on the island's natural resources."

An age-old debate that wouldn't further Ryan's

cause, so instead he asked, "Did you grow up on Maui?"

"Yes," came the curt reply.

"Have you ever lived anywhere else?"

"Oahu, for college."

Not having explored any of the other islands, he said, "I hear it's much different there than here."

"Yeah. More crowded."

So much for small talk. Ryan kept silent until Nik pulled into the Mana Kai parking lot. "I'm sure I'll be seeing you around," Ryan said.

Nik's black eyes narrowed. "When are you leaving?"

Ryan shrugged. "When my business is done."

"I wouldn't get too set on buying the Kaapa Flower Farm."

"Why's that?"

"Kiki loves the land and Auntie Lana loves Kiki."

The bond between the two women had been obvious and Ryan really admired that they had a close relationship. His own grandparents were long gone. "Pano seems to think his grandmother should sell."

"But Pano doesn't have the same attachment to the farm as Kiki nor the same sway as Kiki. Kiki's mother is Lana's only child. Pano's mother was from Uncle Kaapa's first marriage."

"Oh." Ryan hadn't known that and really doubted that Tutu would harbor any favoritism of Kiki over Pano because he wasn't her blood grandson. Kiki worked hard on the farm and in caring for her grand-mother. That counted a lot, in Ryan's book.

He got out of the car. "Thanks for the ride."

Nik gave a nod and drove away.

When Ryan entered his condo, there was a message on the answering machine from Horatio Lewis wanting to know how soon the deal would be wrapped up.

He tried to dismiss the uneasiness clouding his judgment. With pipe bombs exploding, a letter with threats and a beautiful, stubborn, vulnerable woman all crowding his brain, he had a hard time concentrating on what he should be doing. Getting a signature on the contract.

Ryan called back and left his own message, saying he'd have more news come Monday.

And if all went well, hopefully, the news would be good.

On the hillside facing the Kaapa Flower Farm, beneath a strand of hala trees, their saw-toothed, bent leaves a perfect place to hide, a man watched Kiki Brill go about the task of watering the crops. Her graceful hands and lean, muscled arms bunched as she turned the spigot that would send water flowing through the pipes laid out along the roots of the flowering plants and lush foliage.

Frustration beat a steady rhythm at his temple. The explosion yesterday hadn't sufficiently scared her. He'd have to step up his methods. He needed her to be scared. Wanted her scared. And he'd destroy the whole Kaapa Farm if that's what it took.

Later that evening, before entering the Kaapa house, Ryan paused to slip off his shoes, honoring the Hawaiian culture's sign of respect and humility. He left them just outside the door. Lana Kaapa waited for him with the screen door held wide, her long, embroidered dress as bright and welcoming as her round, remarkably unlined face.

"Ryan, so glad you could come," she said with a broad smile.

He held out the plate of oatmeal-raisin cookies he'd made earlier that afternoon in his condo's little kitchen. A nod to another Hawaiian custom of bringing food to your host when visiting.

Lana took the plate and urged him inside. "These look homemade. You?"

"My mother's recipe."

"Kiki, look what Ryan brought us." Lana headed toward the kitchen, where Kiki was busy cooking.

Ryan set his briefcase by the door and absorbed the warmth and amazing smells that enveloped him.

"Thank you, Ryan, that was very thoughtful," Kiki stated, her dark gaze resting on him for a moment before she turned back to her task.

"Have a seat, Ryan," Lana said, indicating the dining-room chairs. "Would you like something to drink?"

"Whatever you have cold would be great, Auntie Lana."

Lana nodded, her eyes dancing at his use of Auntie. His mother raised him right, and it was only right to acquaint yourself with what was proper when you visited people of another culture. Plus, it made good business sense.

Ryan took a seat on a cane-back chair that wobbled beneath him. For a moment he thought the piece of furniture would break. And he wasn't that heavy.

On closer inspection, he noticed that one of the legs had a split running vertically up to the base. The thing could very well collapse out from under him. He braced his feet firmly on the floor, ready to catch himself if need be.

"And you may call me Tutu," Lana said with a smile as she returned with a tall glass of juice on ice.

From the kitchen, Kiki made a noise that sounded suspiciously like a choking cough. Ryan glanced up. Her expression left him no doubt she didn't appreciate her grandmother's offer of familiarity. No surprise there.

He drank the sweet juice, recognizing the passionfruit, orange, guava drink as what the locals called POG.

Kiki came to the dining area, wiping her slender hands on a towel. "You could make yourself useful and help me in the kitchen."

He rose from his rickety seat, surprised and oddly

pleased by the request. "I'm at your service. Where can I wash up?"

"The bath is down the hall on the left."

When he reentered the living room with clean hands, he heard the most enchanting singing in the kitchen. Kiki. With quick and efficient movements she chopped up a chunk of raw meat as she sang.

Impressed, he quietly approached the counter to listen. The words were in Hawaiian and the tune unfamiliar, but her voice mesmerized him.

"E Hawai`i, e ku`u one hanau e,
Ku`u home kulaiwi nei
`Oli no au in na pono lani ou.
E Hawai`I, aloha e!"

"A classic song of the islands," Lana said softly as she joined him. "She'll sing and hula at the Aloha Festival next weekend."

Hula? Now that would be interesting to see Kiki do. She'd be graceful, yes, but considering how tightly coiled she appeared to be, he had a hard time envisioning her moving so freely. "I hope I'm around to see it."

But if things went well for him, he wouldn't be.

Lana patted his arm. "Me, too."

The urge to ask her to consider the offer he'd brought rose sharply. He bit his tongue, choosing to wait to talk about the purchase of the land until after dinner. He did wonder, though, if Tutu really didn't want to sell or if Kiki was standing in the way of closing the deal.

A spurt of anxiety hit Ryan square in the chest. What would happen to Tutu and Kiki if they did sell?

FIVE

Ryan mentally snorted. They'd receive a huge fortune and could live in high style anywhere they wanted.

He entered the kitchen, and Kiki stopped singing. She turned to face him. Her brown-gold eyes conveyed a moment of embarrassment before turning as dark as hardened lava. The momentary glimpse of the chink in her armor made tenderness rise in his chest.

"Are you up for cutting the taro root?" she asked him.

"Sure." He had no idea what taro root was, but how hard could it be? He entered the limited space of the kitchen, aware of Kiki's subtle floral scent that the man in him picked out over the smells of the prepared food.

Kiki handed him a bottle of olive oil. "Pour this over your hands or the root will irritate your skin."

"Irritate as in annoy, or as in sticking my hands in battery acid?"

She rolled her eyes. "Somewhere in between."

"Okay." He did as instructed, lubricating his palms and fingers liberally with the oil. He lifted his gaze to find Kiki's avid eyes on him. She blinked and quickly thrust a paring knife handle into his hand, which he quickly fumbled.

"Careful," she said.

"Easier said than done with oil-slick hands," he quipped. Gripping the small knife's black handle proved challenging.

"Here." Kiki set out several taro roots for him to skin and cut.

As it turned out, the tubular vegetable had a hairy outer coating similar to a coconut and was just as tricky to strip. Using the paring knife, he peeled back the layers of coating to reveal the yellowish inner part. He put the edible sections in a bowl she'd placed before him, then retrieved the garbage from beneath the sink and cleared the cutting board and counter with a sweep of his hand.

"Anything else?" He waited for his next task, liking the fact that they could at least cook together. Maybe she'd loosen up enough for him to convince her to sell the property.

Kiki pushed at the stray strands of dark hair that had escaped her braid and shook her head. "I'm just going to stir-fry this meat and add it to the stew and that will be that."

"I'll go clean myself up," he said, and headed back to the bathroom. The oil proved difficult to remove, but after scrubbing with the hard white bar of soap, he finally decided he'd washed enough.

When he rejoined the ladies, Pano had arrived. Obviously Tutu had made good her promise to Nik to have her grandson come stay with them, because two big duffel bags rested on the faded couch.

"Hey, Haole," Pano said, and clapped him on the back.

"Pano," Ryan acknowledged him. "Thanks for the lessons today."

"Not a problem. You did well." Pano went into the kitchen to lift the lid on the stew. Kiki swatted him away and set him to putting together a salad, which he soon brought over to the table.

Avoiding the chair with the split, Ryan sat in the chair facing the kitchen. From his vantage point he could watch Kiki as she ladled the stew into bowls before handing the bowls to her grandmother. He liked the way her straight nose tipped upward slightly at the end and the graceful way she moved. He could watch her all day.

All work and no play was taking its toll on him. He needed to *not* get caught up in her.

Ryan's gaze was drawn away from Kiki as Lana set a bowl in front of him and one in front of Pano as he sat down. When Pano picked up his spoon, aiming for the bowl, his grandmother cuffed him gently on the side of the head. "Mind your manners."

Pano set the spoon down and heaved a sigh. To

Ryan he said, "We don't eat until everyone has been served and grace said."

"Ah. Like the house I grew up in." He met Kiki's approving gaze. "Asking for God's blessing is a sacred affair."

When the ladies were seated, Pano clasped Ryan's hand and Lana's.

Ryan took Kiki's hand. It was a welcome sensation for a moment. Until he realized how well her finely sculpted palm fit against his and her fingers curled with warmth, chasing away all awareness except for where their hands met.

His response to her touch unnerved him. How could he feel such a closeness with someone by just holding her hand?

Must be because of the events of the last two days. An explosion, a threatening letter. Not the average workweek. Definitely things that brought people closer together. He was getting pulled into her world when all he wanted to do was cut a deal and return to his own world, his own life.

Ryan said a silent amen as Lana finished a prayer of blessing over their food and thanksgiving for their guest. Pano released his hand. But Ryan held on to Kiki's for a moment, not wanting to break the physical connection.

Her gaze searched his face, her eyes wide and her mouth slightly parted. Then she frowned as confusion clouded her eyes. Ryan released her hand and quickly picked up his spoon to taste the savory-smelling dish in front of him.

"Mmm. This is delicious. What is it again?" Ryan asked.

"Pau`u stew. Pork shoulder with taro root, carrots, celery, bay leaf, garlic, a touch of curry and other seasonings," Kiki answered.

"Kiki makes the best dishes," Pano said. "Even when we were kids, she was always in the kitchen cooking. Of course, now she only wastes her time on the farm slaving away."

"The best way to a man's heart is through his stomach," quipped Lana, ignoring Pano's last comment.

Kiki choked on her food. She threw Ryan a quick glance. "Tutu."

Lana Kaapa smiled sweetly. "That's how I snagged your Tutukani. He loved my cooking."

Ryan sure loved Kiki's cooking. Not that he was snagged or anything.

"We all love your cooking, Tutu," Kiki remarked.

Pano stretched and said, "You know you'd both have more time to cook if the farm didn't take so much time and energy from you."

Ryan should give the guy a medal for paving the way to talk about the new offer for the land.

Kiki pinned her cousin with a stare. "You don't know what you're talking about."

Pano set down his spoon and folded his hands together, looking as if he was settling in for a fight. It was like watching a train wreck coming. Ryan wanted to intervene, but this was a family squabble. He knew better than to get in the middle of those kinds of issues. Meddling wouldn't further his own plan of talking the Kaapa women into selling.

"Don't I?" Pano asked, the hurt in his expression evident. "You act like you're the only one who cares, Kiki. This is a perfect time for McClain to tell Tutu about the offer he's brought."

"We are not selling. I'm going to make the farm profitable." There was an undercurrent of anger in her quiet voice. "I can't believe you want to push Tutu from her home."

Pano rolled his eyes. "You're so melodramatic. I want Tutu to enjoy the rest of her life rather than watch you tank the farm."

Seeing how upset Kiki was, Ryan's hand clenched as protective instincts surged. He resisted. He had to think of his own agenda and not champion Kiki right now. But he hated to see anyone taking verbal hits.

Kiki stood. "I'm not going to tank the farm. How could you say that? I'm going to make it work."

Pano shook his head, the disbelief clear on his broad face. "No, you're not. You're going to ruin it just like you did with that Web business you started."

Kiki sputtered. "I… How dare you. You…you know nothing about that."

Neither did Ryan. He'd somehow missed noting

a previously failed business venture during his re-search on the family. Interesting.

Pano scoffed with just the barest hint of bitterness lacing his words. "I know your daddy put up a bunch of money for you to lose. Not everyone has a rich papa to dole out money to play with."

"That is enough, Pano," Lana reprimanded in a tight voice.

Tears shimmering in her beautiful eyes, Kiki stormed out of the house. Every instinct in Ryan screamed for him to go after her. He rose intent to offer her what comfort he could when Lana's hand on his arm halted him.

Lana sighed. "I'm sorry, Ryan, you had to witness our little family drama."

"Please, no need to apologize. Believe me I know, when it comes to family, money and responsibilities, emotions tend to run high." At least they did in his family.

Pano sat back in his chair, which squeaked beneath his bulk. Ryan anticipated any moment the chair would give.

"So what is your offer, McClain?"

Ryan eyed Pano then turned to Mrs. Kaapa. His mind was on Kiki, but he couldn't turn down the opening he'd been praying for. "I do have a *very* lucrative offer in my briefcase. Would *you* be interested in looking at the papers?"

"Of course she would," Pano responded.

A spurt of irritation at Pano's high-handedness ran through Ryan. Weird, since they both apparently had the same goal in mind.

Ryan should be glad that at least the one man in the Kaapa family wasn't as attached to the land as the women. But he didn't like to see anyone bullied.

But why should it matter?

This was just business, nothing personal.

"Why don't you leave the papers and I'll look them over. We can talk on Monday," Lana said.

"That's more than fair." Ryan left the table and retrieved his briefcase. He opened the case and took out the file folder with the documents. He had a duplicate in his condo. "My card is in here with my cell number."

Lana took the folder just as Pano reached for it. Maybe she had Pano's number after all.

Pano shrugged and stood. "I'm gonna go watch TV."

"Can I help with the dishes?" Ryan asked, and tried to keep from throwing Pano a disapproving glare. Ryan's mother had made certain her children knew they were to carry their weight in chores no matter where they were, guest or not.

Lana's smile showed her appreciation. "That's very thoughtful of you, Ryan. You can help me clear the table."

Ryan carried the used bowls and utensils to the counter while Lana deftly handled the rest. Through the small window above the sink, the cloudless night appeared full of shadows. Uneasiness slithered across his shoulders, tensing the muscles.

A pipe bomb had been planted in a fertilizer truck here, probably on a night exactly like this one. And Kiki was outside in the dark by herself. Not good. Not good at all.

"I'll say good-night, now, Tutu," Ryan said, turning away from the window and moving to where Tutu stood. On impulse, he leaned close to kiss the older woman's cheek before heading out the door.

After slipping his shoes back on, he walked across the wooden porch, which creaked beneath him, the sound spreading chills along his arms. While he descended the short flight of stairs, a small gecko scurried along the handrail, blending perfectly with the wood.

His gaze searched the darkness for Kiki and found her instantly recognizable silhouette at the end of the drive. In the glow of the half-moon, Ryan could see she was talking to a stooped man holding a white billy goat on a rope.

The agitation in the animated conversation taking place between Kiki and the goat's owner was unmistakable. Curious and a bit concerned, even though the man was elderly, Ryan strode past his rented white Mustang toward the pair. He stopped far enough away for a semblance of privacy but close enough to hear what was going on.

"I understand, Uncle Laanui, but we are not ready to give up on the business."

The elderly man said something in Hawaiian that Ryan didn't understand. Kiki's back stiffened and her fisted hands came to rest on her hips. "Threats won't make me change my mind."

The man stomped off down the driveway with the goat in tow.

Ryan quickly closed the distance between them. "He threatened you?"

She spun toward him, her braid swinging like a pendulum. "With old superstitions. Nothing to fear."

Ryan stared at the spot where the night had closed over the old man. "This Laanui just happened to be out walking his goat?"

She made a noise in her throat. "More like he was probably getting ready to let the goat loose in the crops. Again."

Ryan searched her moon-kissed face, touched by the shadows of the night. She wasn't kidding. "You need to tell Nik. Maybe the old man had something to do with your truck exploding and the note you found."

"Maybe." She searched his face much as he'd searched hers, but with their height difference, he doubted she'd see anything but shadows. Her huff of frustration as she turned away made him believe he'd been right.

She swung to face him again. "I still don't know why you care so much. Especially when you've been conspiring with the neighbors for so long and I didn't know."

"*Conspiring* is such a negative word," Ryan commented, though he couldn't deny the prick of guilt he felt because he had been doing just that. "I left the documents for the offer with your grandmother."

The flash of anger in Kiki's eyes was obvious. He held up his hand before she could say anything. "You already agreed that it wouldn't hurt to at least look at the offer."

Her shoulders slumped slightly. "I know I did. That doesn't mean I have to like it."

The sudden squawk of a bird rousted from its nest filled the night sky. Kiki jerked, turning toward the hillside. The hairs on the back of Ryan's neck tingled. He didn't much like the feeling. He quickly put an arm around Kiki and led her back toward the house.

"Probably just a nightjar robbing a nest," Kiki said, though her tone wasn't exactly confident.

He kept his tone light despite the way he was feeling. "Not a billy goat?"

She glanced back down the road. "No. Not a goat."

Ryan propelled her up the stairs and into the light of the porch. "Nightjar?"

"A nocturnal bird of prey," she replied, her gaze searching the dark countryside.

"Pardon the pun, but you and Tutu are sitting ducks in this house. On Monday, you're going to call about getting a security system in place here," Ryan said.

Kiki's gaze slid to his. Fire sparked in the golden depths. "I am, am I?"

"Yes. It's unfair for you to allow Tutu to be in any kind of danger," he replied, playing the one card he knew she couldn't trump.

Her lips parted in indignation, then pressed into a thin line.

Time to retreat before he stepped way over the line of professionalism and gave her a lecture in safety. His sister always hated when Ryan or his brothers lectured her. Ryan suspected their concerned opinions usually pushed Meg to do the exact opposite.

He had a feeling in this situation even his sister would agree with taking precautions, but for now he'd let Kiki think on it. She'd see he was right.

Taking her hand, he kissed the knuckles. "I'll see you in the morning for church."

Her eyes widened. "Right. Church." She slipped her hand away and stepped toward the door. "Good night, Ryan."

He waited until she'd entered the house and slid the lock home. He made his way to his rental car, the whole while his gaze searching the shadowy darkness for any hidden threat.

"Please, Lord, protect the Kaapa family," he whispered, and hoped the nightjar was the only creature on the prowl in the inky blackness of the night.

* * *

Sunday morning, Kiki and Tutu arrived at Ryan's condo in Kiki's little car just a little before nine. Leaving Tutu sitting in the passenger seat, Kiki took the elevator to the fourth floor to get Ryan. She put her hand on her abdomen to cover the fluttery excitement in the pit of her stomach.

In the mirrored reflection of the elevator walls, she checked that her sundress hung properly and that her light colored lip gloss wasn't smeared on her teeth.

Though why she was so nervous she didn't know. It wasn't as if this was a date. They were going to church.

When he opened the door, giving her his devastating grin, her breath hitched in her chest and made her glad she'd chosen to take such care with her own appearance. His dark hair had been combed into submission and his jaw clean-shaven. He wore light colored, pleat-front twill pants and a navy pin-striped button-down shirt. Handsome. Very yuppie *GQ*. Very mainlander.

In his hand he held a red-and-blue-striped piece of cloth. "To tie or not to tie?"

Staying at the threshold of the door, she shook her head. "No tie."

"Okay, then." He tossed the strip of fabric onto a chair and grabbed his wallet and keys off the table before joining her in the hall.

As they made their way to the elevator, his hand settled on the small of her back as if he'd been touching her for years. Kiki tried not to let his presence bother her. But how could she not be aware of him, when every fiber of her being went on alert whenever he came near?

Last night she'd known the moment he'd stepped out of the house despite the distance between them. She had sensed his every move as he'd walked down the darkened driveway. She normally didn't believe in a sixth sense, but with him, maybe it was possible.

On their way down to the main floor, she tried her best not to stare at their reflection in the door, but since the entire interior of the small space was mirrored it was hard not to notice how well they looked together.

She was glad when the elevator doors opened and she stepped out into the fresh air where she could catch her breath. Ryan greeted Tutu as he climbed in to the backseat of the VW. The drive to the church took only a few minutes.

"What is that?" Ryan pointed to a strange-looking rodent with a long body and just as long tail that darted out into the street and then back under a hibiscus bush.

Kiki's lip curled. "That's a mongoose. They're a bit of a problem."

Tutu added, "They originally were brought over by sugarcane mill owners who wanted a way to control the rats on the islands, but unfortunately, they didn't take into consideration that rats are nocturnal and mongoose aren't."

"Ah, I can see how that would be a problem."

Kiki brought the car to a halt in the parking lot of the church alongside a jacaranda tree. The tree's cheery purple buds always made her smile.

Kiki, Tutu and Ryan headed to the large barnlike structure which sat imposingly on an incline. The pristine white exterior made the red-trimmed windows and doors seem that much more vibrant.

A white steeple rose from the roofline, and a tall white cross gleamed against the backdrop of the blue sky. Lava rocks were stacked to form a path leading to the arched overhang where parishioners gathered to greet the kahuna, Pastor Gerome, in his long white robe that covered his bulky frame. She noticed Pano and his friends enter ahead of them.

"Aloha! *Pehea`oe,* Auntie Lana?" Pastor Gerome said as he took Tutu's hands.

"*Maika`i,* Pastor. You remember Kiki?"

"Aloha, Kiki." He took her hand and gave it a squeeze before turning his attention to Ryan. "And your *ho`aloha?*"

Her friend? Not so much. Well, maybe. "Pastor Gerome, this is Ryan McClain. He's visiting from the mainland," Kiki replied.

The two men shook hands.

"Yes, so I've heard," stated the pastor.

Kiki frowned. "You've heard?"

He smiled indulgently at her. "We are a small congregation. There are many who would like to see the land developed and there are many who would not."

He shifted his gaze to Ryan. "You have created a stir among the neighbors."

"So I understand," Ryan replied, his expression somber and respectful.

"We are glad you are here with us today anyway."

"Thank you, sir."

Kiki grimaced at Ryan's use of the formal word that had no place in the Hawaiian language, but the kahuna didn't seem offended.

Ryan laid a hand on Kiki's arm as they moved down the aisle to find a seat. "What nationality is the pastor?"

She narrowed her gaze on him, irritated by his question and by the sudden suspicion that he held some prejudice. It was exactly the kind of question her grandfather Brill would ask. "I don't know. I've never thought about it."

She glanced over her shoulder to study the kahuna. His weathered face beamed with kindness as he shook hands with those coming in. His skin was brown like most people from the South Pacific region, and his dark eyes were slanted slightly, indicating some Asian influence, yet his black hair had an African texture.

She trained her gaze back on Ryan. "Does it matter?"

Ryan shook his head. "Not in the least. I like him. He seems very genuine." Ryan slid onto the wooden pew next to Tutu.

Relieved by his answer, Kiki nodded in agreement. But the pastor's words about there being many who would like the land developed and many who wouldn't, bothered her.

She didn't like that her family's business was being discussed so freely among the populace. Or that so *many* people had a stake in whether the Kaapa Flower Farm was sold or not. She glanced around.

Were those whose gazes she met staring back because she'd brought a malihini, a visitor, and a Haole, at that, to church? Or was there some other reason for their stares? Had someone here planted the pipe bomb and the letter? Or was one of the men she didn't recognize Jeff Tolar? The picture her father had e-mailed had shown an older man with shaggy, dirty-blond hair and a darker graying beard. Kiki didn't know if she'd be able to pick him out in a crowd without his facial hair. He could easily change his appearance and be anyone.

With a shudder of apprehension, she tried to focus as she made her way to the stage for the worship part of the service, but her mind kept going back to the danger that seemed to lurk so close.

Would a security system, as Ryan and Nik had suggested, be able to stop someone from destroying the farm if they were really determined to do so?

SIX

Sitting in a pew about ten rows back from the altar, Ryan was grateful for the open windows that allowed the trade winds to breeze through the interior of the church. The heavy humid air made his dress shirt cling to his back.

He was surprised when Kiki left her seat to move to the altar just as music filled the sanctuary. He watched in fascination as Kiki, along with three other women, told the story of the hymns the congregation was singing in the form of a hula. He'd been right. Graceful, controlled. Stunning.

But the dance wasn't the commercial, fast-paced frenzied hula one usually thought of, but rather a lyrical expression of hand and body movements that mesmerized and spoke to his soul as he watched the elegant way Kiki swayed, her floral skirt swirling, her body full of tightly controlled energy. She exuded beauty in all its forms. When the music ended, he'd clapped enthusiastically along with everyone else.

When Pastor Gerome took to the stage and instructed the assembly to follow along in their Bibles as he spoke from the book of Joshua, Ryan noticed that Kiki seemed preoccupied as she came back to her place beside him. He reached over to help her flip the pages of her leather Bible. She nodded her thanks, but her gaze didn't go to the page of text but rather searched through the crowd.

Ryan nudged her and leaned in to whisper, "You okay?"

She turned her gold-specked, troubled eyes to him. Two lines formed between her eyebrows as she mouthed the word, *yes.*

Ryan was sure she wasn't being honest but now was not the time to push her. Instead he gave his attention to the sermon.

"Verse 6 states, Be strong and of good courage," Pastor Gerome read from the first chapter. "This phrase occurs four times in this chapter. Look at verses 7, 9 and 18."

Ryan scanned the verses. The phrase was repeated. Interesting.

"This was God's encouragement to Joshua concerning his future tasks," the pastor continued. "And today, we can take encouragement from God's command. Is there a problem you face, a task you must do? 'Be strong and of good courage,' declares the Lord. Trust in the promise of His abiding presence.

Take a look with me as we read of God's words to Joshua after the death of Moses."

Ryan read the words over again. *Be strong and of good courage.*

How did these words relate to his life? A problem he faced, a task he must do? Sure, he faced the problem of how to convince Kiki and Tutu to sell their land. But he doubted that what God had in mind was a business-oriented "problem."

He shrugged off the question, but he tucked the verse away just in case one day he needed the encouragement.

He turned his attention back to Kiki, watching as she nervously picked at the fingernail on her right thumb, which he noted was already so short the quick was visible. He placed his hand over hers, stilling the nervous gesture. She acknowledged him with a nod as she trained her gaze ahead.

As Ryan began to shift his hand away, Kiki clasped on, her fingers wrapping around his. Surprised, pleased and a bit apprehensive at the potential meaning of her action—a meaning he wasn't sure he should or wanted to consider—Ryan held her hand through the rest of the service.

The service ended with more hula worship, only this set was more upbeat and left the congregation smiling and clapping. Ryan, Kiki and Tutu filed out of the church along with everyone else.

The humid air hit him in the face, stealing his

breath for a moment. He was glad he hadn't worn the tie. He rolled up the sleeves of his shirt. He would have to buy himself a Hawaiian shirt soon and some T-shirts, since most of the clothing he'd brought with him were business-casual appropriate for Boston, not Maui.

Kiki touched his arm to get his attention. "I'm going to ask Pano to take Tutu home so we can start looking at properties."

Ryan glanced around and spied Pano talking with the two men that had been at the beach the day before. "Good idea."

He watched Kiki walk toward her cousin, her flowered skirt swished about her slender ankles and sandaled feet, making it seem as if she glided rather than walked. Her long hair held loosely back with a brightly colored shell clip made a rich blanket over her shoulders. She talked a moment with Pano and then talked with her grandmother before heading back over to Ryan.

"Shall we?" she asked as she tucked her arm through his.

Knowing he shouldn't be spending so much time with her, but unable to prevent the jumble of awareness cascading over him, he placed his hand over hers and enjoyed the feel of her close to him. And he really appreciated that she felt comfortable enough with him to take his arm in such a possessive manner in public. He liked the feeling that they belonged together, when he knew that was the furthest thing from the truth.

Boy, was he in trouble.

As she drove them down the road, Kiki asked, "What did you think of the service?"

"Very interesting. I really enjoyed the worship."

"And the message?"

He shrugged. "Good."

Kiki frowned as she merged from the Piilani Highway onto Mokuleie Highway. They passed fields of pineapple and palm trees, crawled though small communities and headed toward Kahului where they would pick up the Hana Highway traveling to the north point. "Good. That's it?"

"What do you want me to say?" He faced her, but she couldn't determine what his expressionless tone meant. "I found Pastor Gerome a very interesting speaker."

"But what about God's word? Did you find meaning in the message?" she pressed. Though why she cared she had no idea.

"I'm not sure what to say here, Kiki. What exactly are you asking?"

For some reason disappointment embedded itself in her gut. What did she want from him? Feedback? "I don't know. I just found the message very applicable. I'm going to need to stay strong and have courage to accomplish what God has set me to do," she replied.

"Which is?"

"Save my family's farm from financial ruin and keep it going."

"So you're saying God has asked you to turn the Kaapa Flower Farm into a successful business venture?"

She tried not to take offense at the incredulous tone in his voice. He wouldn't understand if she told him of the hours in prayer she'd spent before coming back to the island with the determination to make the flower farm business viable. She'd failed one business attempt before, and it had been devastating. She didn't know if she could take another failure. And this farm meant so, so much more. It didn't just represent what she did, but also who she was.

She wove the car through the thickening traffic as she took the exit for the Hana Highway that would lead them to Haiku, where a family she knew had some undeveloped land. She had no clue whether they would sell or not. She'd leave such details for Ryan to figure out. She just hoped he'd think the area was a better spot for his investors.

"You didn't answer my question," Ryan prodded.

Kiki sighed. "Yes. I do believe that God wants me here on Maui and He's going to bless the farm."

At least that was her prayer.

Ryan sat back and stared at the scenery going by. Now, how could he compete with that?

He frowned. Not him. *His clients.*

How could Ryan convince Kiki that selling the farm would be in her best interest when she was convinced that God had brought her back to the island to make the farm work? Talk about a hurdle to jump.

Kiki turned the car onto a dirt road which wasn't really a road, but more a path barely big enough for the car. He had to admit, as he surveyed the landscape, that this part of the island was beautiful with its flat land gently verging into grassy slopes and the ocean right there in front of them, the waves crashing against the lava-laden shore, creating yet another form of God's music. Not a sandy beach, but still breathtaking.

Kiki brought the car to a halt at the end of the path. "This land belongs to the Okano family. Wouldn't a resort here be perfect?"

He suppressed a chuckle at the coaxing note in her voice. "It is amazing. Though I think my investors like the mountainous view, as well as the ocean views."

"But this is right on the water. Listen to the waves. Wouldn't you think resort guests would find the sound of the crashing surf soothing? And the town of Haiku is very quaint with some very nice restaurants and shops."

She was trying so hard and he hated to disappoint her, but it couldn't be helped. This was just business. "I don't think so. The layout and design plan wouldn't work here."

"You're not even going to check?"

"Kiki, this isn't what the investor envisioned," he stated.

"Well, I know another parcel of land that might be better," she said, and backed the car down the path.

Once back on the highway she flipped on the radio, clearly not wanting to talk. Ryan relaxed back in the seat. At least Kiki was with him. Here in this car, Kiki was safe. And Tutu was with Pano. Being with her beat worrying alone in his condo. The sun's rays heated his skin and the rhythm of the tires eating up the pavement lulled him to sleep.

He was jolted awake when the car hit a bump, bouncing him in his seat. He looked around and realized he must have fallen asleep because the terrain looked nothing like where they had been. Lush, green tropical flora spread across the rugged land. "Where are we?"

"The closest town is Kaupo," Kiki replied as she brought the VW to a halt on the side of a chained-off dirt road. "We'll have to walk from here."

Ryan got out of the car and stretched. A walk sounded good after so much sitting. The trek down the dirt path that wound through the foliage was rife with jutting roots and sharp bits of lava rock embedded in the ground. His dress shoes and her sandals weren't exactly made for the terrain. The humid air made his shirt stick to his back and sweat drip from his hair.

"The Ihe family holds the property rights to this land. There has been talk that the government would like to take ownership, but until the elder Ihe passes on, the family has the right to sell if they choose," Kiki explained.

Spreading her hands wide, she said, "Wouldn't this be a perfect place for a resort? Off the beaten path with beautiful views of Haleakala National Park." She pointed off to the east.

Ryan turned to view the dense greenery that traveled up the mountainous range. "Very picturesque."

Kiki captured his hand and tugged. "Come on. Let's walk down to the beach."

He curled his fingers around hers, liking how natural it felt to have the contact. They made their way through a tunneled overhang of several butterfly bushes all intertwined. They emerged out the other side onto a U-shaped cove with a short stretch of sandy beach. Ocean waves lapped at the boulders made of lava rock dotting the shore.

"See. Isn't this wonderful? If you built the resort on this parcel of land, there would be a private beach to go with it. We only have a cove, no beach," she said, her expression eager and earnest. "This is exactly what your investors are envisioning. Mountain views and a beach."

He couldn't stop himself from running the pad of his thumb over her knuckles. "How many acres are here?"

She tugged on her bottom lip. "Uh, well, I'm not exactly sure. I think maybe thirteen or so."

"It's beautiful."

"So you'll see if your investors would be interested in this parcel of land?"

The hope in her voice made his chest tighten. He wished he could tell her what she wanted to hear. "I don't think it's big enough, for one. Two, and I may be wrong, but I'm not sure the Hawaii building codes would allow construction so close to a national park. And three, there's no fresh water piped here, like there is to the Kaapa land."

Disappointment showed in her eyes and the slump of her shoulders. "We better get back, then."

She slipped her hand from his. He had to let her go.

Ryan followed Kiki back through the butterfly bush, hustling to keep up with her as she stalked back toward where they'd left the car. Kiki had pulled out ahead a good two feet in front of him when she came to an abrupt halt. As he closed the distance between them, the air thickened with the fumes of gasoline.

The foreboding that had gripped him the night before at her kitchen window gave way to a fierce protectiveness. He touched Kiki arms as he passed her. "Stay put."

Cautiously, he approached the car for inspection. He crouched to look at the undercarriage. Anger, hot and heavy, breathed down his neck. He stood up and backed away from the dizzying fumes. They were a long way from the Kaapa Flower Farm, but first a pipe bomb, then a threatening note, now this?

"Someone has cut the fuel line," he announced, his voice echoing in the still air.

He took out his cell phone. No signal alert. He ground his teeth in frustration.

"Kiki, can you see if you have a signal?" He turned to find her staring transfixed at the car. The terrified expression arrested on her lovely face sent concern racing through him. He rushed to her side. "Kiki?"

"Would it have blown up if I'd started it?" she asked, her voice wobbly.

"Not likely. Whoever did this would have known there was no way we'd get in with the smell of fuel so strong."

"But what if we hadn't smelled the fumes?" she insisted.

"Still unlikely, unless…"

"Unless?"

He shrugged. "Unless there was more tampering."

Kiki shuddered and wrapped her arms around herself. "Do you think whoever planted the pipe bomb and the note did this?"

He saw where her thought process was going. "I just don't see it. We're miles from the flower farm. How would damaging your car help in the sicko's quest to frighten you into selling?"

"I was afraid of that," she said, and edged closer to him while her gaze searched the surrounding area as if at any moment she expected someone to jump out and attack them. "We're awfully isolated here. Fish in a tide pool. I really didn't think I mattered."

Taking her by the shoulders and holding her attention, he said, "Tell me what has you so spooked. What is going on?"

The gold flecks in her eyes seemed to darken with anxiety. "There's been a threat made against the Brill family. Specifically, the grandkids. Apparently the ex-con whom my grandfather—who's a judge by the way—put away has sworn revenge."

A boulder-sized knot of fear lodged in his gut. "No wonder you're freaked out."

He rubbed her arms, trying to soothe her, as well as himself. He scanned the road and bushes in both directions. They'd been followed, but hadn't seen another soul, and the only sound he could pick out was the distant crash of the surf. "Does Nik know about this?"

She shook her head. "My father said he'd contact the local police. I only found out right after the explosion the other day."

Again protective instincts roared through him like a wolf defending his pack. "Wow. Okay. That definitely puts a different spin on the situation. First thing tomorrow I'm going to make sure we get you some sort of a security system installed—" He held up a hand to prevent the protest forming on her lips. "No arguments. But first we have to get out of here. Check your cell. I have no service."

Kiki unhooked her cell phone from the clip at her waist. "Me, neither."

Just as he feared. "Looks like we're hoofing it to the nearest phone. Which way?"

"This way." She pointed left. "At Mile Marker #35 there's a small store in Kaupo. They should have a landline we can use."

Setting out toward the Kaupo store, he and Kiki fell into step on the paved but neglected road. A slight trade wind kicked up, stirring the humid air and making the baking tropical sun more tolerable.

"Can you tell me about the Brill family?" Ryan asked as a way to distract them both from the situation and its implications.

Gamely, she said, "The Brills have been in Philadelphia since the founding fathers. My grandfather is a judge, just as his father before him. My father is the only one of my grandparents' kids who went into law, but I have two cousins who have ambitions to follow in Grandfather's footsteps."

"What about your parents?"

"Dad came to the island right after he graduated from Harvard." A smile touched her lips. "My mother was dancing in the Aloha Festival when my father first laid eyes on her. He likes to say he fell in love instantly without even knowing her, but mother says they were inseparable for the next seven days, and on the eighth day, my father proposed. They were married as soon as a license could be procured, right here on the island."

"How very romantic." And very impulsive. A trait he would never attribute to Kiki. He liked that she was steady, committed and conventional. A woman whom a man could count on, no matter the circumstances.

"My grandparents were livid. They had a debutante already picked out as their daughter-in-law. My dad went against his parents' wishes to marry for love."

"A wise choice. One should love the one they're married to," Ryan commented, as he stepped over a root that had broken through the pavement. His parents had shared a deep love, or so his siblings told him. An ache throbbed in his heart. How could he feel a loss of something he'd never known?

Kiki sighed. "Yes, I suppose that's true."

Her pessimistic expression belied her words. "You don't believe in love?"

"I do. I just…have been burned before. Not an experience I intend to repeat."

Curiosity wrapped around him. What idot would burn an amazing woman like Kiki? "Want to tell me about it?"

Glancing over her shoulder, she said, "Not especially."

They walked in silence for a stretch. Along the inland side of the unevenly paved road, the foliage grew thick and abundant. Fronds swayed and crackled gently in the trade wind. On the ocean side of the road the cliffs grew more steep and rugged. The deep blue hues of the Pacific Ocean stretched to meet the bright pale sky, creating a visible horizon line.

No other humans were around, which should be reassuring, but the feeling left Kiki unsettled. Having her car tampered with was enough to make her heart pound; she didn't need to add the creepy impression of isolation to the mix. The silence between them only exaggerated the sensation. While she might not want to air out her romantic skeletons, she did itch to know more about Ryan. "So, tell me about your life in Boston," she asked. "What do you do for fun?"

"I work."

She arched an eyebrow at him. "That's it? How about a girlfriend?"

A dry laugh escaped Ryan. "I don't have time for love right now."

She didn't understand why she was glad he wasn't taken. Refusing to study her reaction, she focused on what he'd just said, "What does that mean?"

Ryan shrugged. "I have goals and those goals require executing certain plans. Love and family and all that will come in the future, but at the present time, I'm committed to my work, to amassing my wealth so I can afford to have a family."

For some reason his answer didn't surprise her, but also made her feel slightly sad. "So you think you can plan love? Just one day say, 'Okay it's time to find someone to love' and bam, it happens?"

He gave her a sidelong glance. "You make it sound so… I'm not sure even how to describe it."

An unreasonable dose of irritation gripped her. She chalked the sensation up to the events of the day. Not only hadn't he been interested in the properties she'd shown him, but now he was talking about amassing a wealth that would come at her family's expense. "Sounds pretty controlling to me. What if God has other plans? Do you just ignore Him for your own agenda?"

He tugged at the collar of his dress shirt. "I'm sure my agenda and God's will line up."

She stopped walking. "So you will ask God for guidance?"

He stopped, as well. "Yeah, sure," he replied, but his tone wasn't very confident.

Though he'd already stated he went to church and grew up in a Christian home, she wanted to know where he stood in his faith, though why it mattered she didn't know. "Do you ask for God's guidance now?"

"Yes." He frowned. "Sort of."

Not sure what the wishy-washy statement meant, she said, "I ask God for guidance all the time because I know I can't get through this life without Him." She started walking again, her thoughts and her tone turning introspective. "I do question sometimes why life has to be so hard, though. And painful."

"God's word never promised life would be easy."

Surprised by his assessment and pleased that he sounded so sure, she replied, "True. Have you read much of the Bible?"

"Yes. Memorizing scripture was a big part of the Sunday School lesson every week when I was a kid," he replied.

"Knowing the words in your head isn't the same has having them in your heart," she commented quietly.

"You sound like everyone else in my family."

She wasn't sure how to respond to that. Obviously, his family suspected his faith didn't run very deep. Normally, she felt that each person was entitled to deepen their faith in their own time in their own way. But it hurt her heart to think of Ryan's faith being shallow and vulnerable to the world's temptations.

He already put so much stock in material wealth, which she knew didn't bring happiness or peace. Her Brill family had more money in their coffers than could be spent in their lifetimes, yet none were really content with their lives.

She hated to think of Ryan spending his life striving for something that could so easily be his if he'd only give himself over to God. She wanted to help him strengthen his belief and make him see that try-ing to control the future wasn't fruitful. But words stuck in her throat. She wasn't an evangelist. And why should Ryan's faith matter to her anyway?

Mentally, she chastised herself—everyone's faith mattered. Ryan was no exception. She didn't know what to say to him, though. Silence sometimes was the best response.

"Pano mentioned a Web business you started. What happened there?" he asked, his tone interested.

The change in topic was a relief on one hand, yet managed to bring an instant flush of irritation to her cheeks. She rolled her eyes. "Pano has a big mouth. And he doesn't know what he's talking about. I didn't ruin it. I had a partner. It was the partnership that didn't work out, so we dissolved the business."

"Is this partner the one who burned you in a love relationship?"

Kiki caught the toe of her sandal on the pavement. How had he guessed that? Had her tone given her away? She could feel his intense gaze studying her profile. She raised her chin a notch. "Yes."

"What happened?"

"He was a lying, cheating jerk who only wanted access to the Brill fortune." She couldn't keep the bit-terness from creeping into her voice.

"That sucks."

"Yeah, big-time." She walked a bit faster, as if she could outrun the conversation, even though he was bound to ask other questions. Sure, it had hurt to realize Andrew had been more interested in becoming "part of the family" than being with her.

But the pain had turned to anger so quickly, that once he was out of the picture, it was a relief. What did that say about her? She'd been intent on marrying a man she hadn't truly and deeply loved? Here she'd just told Ryan she believed in love, agreed that a marriage should be based on love. What a hypocrite.

And yet, suddenly she was extremely grateful she hadn't married Andrew. God's plans for her obviously hadn't included Andrew. She wouldn't be at the farm she so deeply loved if she'd married him. And that left her feeling freer than she had in a long time.

But not free enough to forget the danger her family faced.

Up ahead on the side of the road a stout square building lounged, tucked between palms, their fronds like feathers, protecting the antique-looking store with its wooden wraparound porch. A beautiful red horse, with a Western saddle and a mane that sported beaded braids stood grazing on the grass near the entrance.

As Kiki and Ryan approached, the beast lifted its head and whinnied. A strip of leather tethered the horse to a hitching post.

"Wow. That's not something you see in Boston. I feel as if I'm in an old Western," Ryan commented.

"He's a beauty," Kiki stated, as she took the stairs to the store entrance.

"Aloha," said a round Polynesian woman from behind the counter.

"Aloha. Our car broke down. Do you have a phone we can use?" Ryan asked as he stepped into the store beside Kiki.

The woman pointed to the corner. A pay phone hung attached to the wall next to a rack of pork rinds and chips.

Kiki headed to the phone with Ryan hot on her heels. "I want to call home first," she told him.

He nodded as he dug into his pants pocket for some change.

She waved the money away. "I'll charge it to the house. I do it all the time."

She dialed and waited for Tutu to pick up. After the fifth ring, just as Kiki was about to hang up, Tutu answered.

"Aloha." Tutu sounded breathless, as if she'd run to get the call.

"Tutu, its Kiki. Is everything all right?"

"Oh, Kiki. I don't know what we're going to do."

Gripping the receiver tight, Kiki asked, her voice shaky, "What's happened?"

"The farm is ruined. We're ruined, Kiki."

SEVEN

Bugs! They had bugs in the fields eating the expensive blooms. Not just any bug, but Japanese beetles. One of the most destructive insects, and one of the hardest to get rid of.

Kiki jumped out of the taxi before it even came to a full stop behind the cars lined up in the driveway of the Kaapa house. With her heart in her throat, she ran to where Tutu and Pano stood near the fence surrounding the flower crop with Nik and another man with shocking white hair that Kiki didn't recognize.

"How could this happen?" she asked as she skidded to a halt.

Tutu gathered Kiki into her arms. "Its just so awful. They're so ugly."

Pano shrugged. "It's not like the place is secure."

Shooting him a glare for pointing out the obvious, Kiki addressed Nik. "What do we do?"

Nik's grim expression didn't bode well. "Pano's right. Anyone can walk right in here at any time."

"Which will be rectified tomorrow," Ryan stated as he joined the group.

Nik slid Ryan a glance, and nodded, then turned his attention back to Kiki. "We found a jar that the bugs were probably released from. I've bagged the jar for examination. We estimate there were at least a couple hundred, possibly more." Gesturing to the man at his side, he said, "This is Gus Hoffman. He's a bug expert."

The stranger stepped forward and extended his thin hand. Gus Hoffman was in his mid to late fifties with intelligent eyes and a rail-thin body, which his gray coveralls accentuated. "I'm an entomologist. Nik asked me to take a look."

Kiki shook his hand. "Thank you for coming. So how do we get rid of them?" Because if they didn't stop them soon, the beetles would eat through the stalks and leaves, rendering this crop worthless. And the larvae would attack the roots, killing the plants and any hope for a crop next year.

Gus rocked back on the heels of his dusty work boots.

"Well, now, there are a few options. Neem spray is a botanical control made from the Indian neem tree. It's somewhat effective. We could treat the soil with Milky Spore, a bacterium that kills the grubs, but that is not a quick fix and since the mature beetles were so recently released they haven't had time to lay eggs.

"So really your best two bets are one, set out some geranium plants, white preferably. There's something in the chemical makeup of the plant that kills the bugs. Or two, pluck them off the plants by hand, which is probably the best option at this point."

Kiki blinked. "By hand?"

Gus nodded. "Yep. Gather as many people and flashlights as you can and when the sun goes down, get out there and pick them off the plants and drown them in a bucket of soapy water."

Her stomach sank with the daunting task. "Great. I guess I can call all the employees and offer them overtime."

How they would find the money she'd worry about later. Could they take another mortgage out on the farm? A call to the bank would be first on her to-do list come Monday.

"I'll help," Ryan said quietly beside her.

She gave him a grateful smile. He'd been a rock for her all day. She was sure he hadn't come to the island thinking he'd be bug picking. But she was extremely thankful he was there. They would need all the hands they could get.

"You're not seriously considering this, are you?" Pano asked, his tone as incredulous as his expression.

Kiki faced him. She was tired of his attitude and wasn't going to let him verbally push her around anymore. "Yes. Are you going to help?"

He scoffed. "That will take hours. And how can you afford to pay anyone regular wages, let alone overtime?"

She didn't know yet, but she didn't want to admit it to her cousin, who clearly wasn't on her side. But at least he wasn't drunk, though she did detect just the faintest whiff of beer on his breath. "We have to do something."

"You could sell," Pano suggested, his voice rife with irony.

Kiki ground her back teeth, seething with anger and turned to plead with her Tutu. "We can't let this be the end of the farm. We have to at least try."

Tutu sighed. "I don't know, dear. This might be a sign from God that it's time to sell."

Outraged, Kiki pulled away from her grand-mother. "No. This was a deliberate act." A thought occurred to her. She spun on Ryan. "The car. Who-ever tampered with the car wanted me to be gone all day so they could do this."

Tutu gasped. "What?"

"That has occurred to me, too," Ryan said, his gaze steady and sharp.

"Your car was tampered with?" Pano stepped for-ward, concern marring his brow. "You weren't hurt, were you?"

Touched that he'd show so much concern, Kiki reached out to touch his arm. "No, just delayed in getting back."

Pano focused on Ryan. "How was the car tampered with?"

Ryan's jaw hardened. "Someone cut the fuel line." His voice echoed with suppressed anger. "Left us stranded near Kaupo."

"Where's the car now?" Pano asked.

Nik spoke up. "It's been towed to the station so the forensic team can look at it."

Nik turned to Gus to shake his hand. "Thanks for coming out here. I appreciate your time."

"No problem." Gus addressed Kiki. "If I can do anything more for you, please let me know. And good luck with your beetles." He sauntered away.

Kiki stared at the acres of crops as despair burdened her shoulders and frustration gurgled in her stomach. How on earth were they going to collect all the bugs before the insects damaged too many of the flowers?

The only saving grace was that none of the beetles had been let loose in her greenhouse. Her precious orchids were safe. She would be buying a padlock for the greenhouse door tomorrow.

Ryan slipped his arm around her shoulders and gave a gentle squeeze. "I'll have Nik take me back to my place. And then I'll round up as many flashlights as I can find in town. You contact your employees."

"Why are you doing this? You should be jumping with joy because this may be what forces us to sell."

She searched his dark eyes for answers, but only saw compassion and resolve.

"Because this isn't the way it should go. You shouldn't be forced to sell, not because someone deliberately set out to make it happen."

It was so nice having someone on her side. "Thank you. I really appreciate you."

He gave her a look full of emotions that she couldn't decipher and then walked away to catch up to Nik just as he was climbing into his rig. She stared after Ryan wondering what that look had meant.

Pano shook his head. "This is a fool's errand, cousin. There's no way we'll get all the bugs."

"But you'll help?" she asked, wondering why he didn't just take off, since he seemed to have such a negative attitude about the farm.

"Of course. I'm a Kaapa, too. I can't let you and Tutu do this alone."

His hurt and offended expression surprised her and filled her with guilt. Of course, he was a Kaapa and of course, he'd want what was best for their Tutu. Just because they didn't agree on what was best didn't make them less of a family. She hugged him. "Thank you."

His big arms engulfed her. "You're welcome. Now, we better start getting things ready. I'll find some buckets and start making the soapy water. You call the workers."

"I'll help you, Kiki," Tutu said as she fell into

step with her granddaughter and headed toward the house. "You should call your father and let him know what's happened today."

Kiki shook her head. "Not yet. Not until I have it all under control."

"Kiki, sometimes reaching out to others is the most courageous thing we can do," Tutu said, her voice full of worry. "Your parents will help if you ask."

"But they have enough to think about with Grandfather's stalker." She didn't want to hurt her grandmother with the truth that her parents would rather Kiki and Lana let the farm go and move to Philadelphia. "And this stunt today wasn't about that. This was about forcing our hand and making sure we sell."

Tutu sighed. "It sure is awfully nice of Ryan to want to help."

"Yes, it is." He'd turned out to be a very nice guy. The kind of guy she'd always dreamed of one day meeting and falling in love with. Only…she'd sworn she wouldn't fall for another mainlander. Especially one who wanted her to sell her heritage.

"He's a good man," Tutu said with a sidelong glance.

Kiki shook her head. "Don't get any ideas, Tutu. He belongs on the mainland and will return to his life soon enough. There's nothing going to happen between Ryan and me." No matter how much she was drawn to him or how much appreciation she felt.

Tutu's little smile didn't bode well. Kiki knew that smile. When her Tutu set her mind on something, she didn't give up. Kiki had inherited that stubbornness.

And it was that stubbornness that would get her through the next few days.

Ryan arrived just as darkness overtook the island; the last of the setting sun's rays disappeared over the horizon with streaks of pale gold fading into the night sky. He'd stopped at a hardware store in downtown Kihei to purchase two dozen flashlights, all the store had on hand. He carried the bag of lights up the porch steps and balanced it on one hip as he knocked.

Kiki opened the door, her warm brown eyes welcoming. "Here, let me take that," she said, relieving him of the bag. She looked inside and gasped with pleasure. "Thank you so much for picking these up."

He slipped off his shoes and entered. The house was filled with people. Young and old. He took a quick head count. Twenty. Impressive. Kiki set the bag on the floor and began handing out the flashlights to those who didn't already have one in hand.

"Everyone, this is Ryan McClain. He's a family friend," Kiki explained.

A pleasant warmth filled him to know she considered him a friend, not foe.

She quickly introduced each person. When she was finished, she said, "So, according to the entomologist, we pluck the beetles off the plants and drown them in a bucket of soapy water. Pano has filled as many buckets as we could find and has placed them at intervals down each line. Here are some plastic bags to use to carry the critters to the buckets."

Tutu handed out the bags as everyone filed out of the house and headed toward the crops.

Ryan fell into step with Kiki. "Are all of these people employees?"

"Most. Some brought their families with them," she said. "I'm so grateful they all agreed to come tonight."

"Will you be able to afford to pay them?"

She shrugged. "I'll find a way. I did explain to them all that payment might be slow in coming but I always repay my debts."

Bottom line, though, would she be able to stay open for business with such an expense? Ryan didn't know their financial situation to the dollar, but he'd done enough research to know they weren't making bank payments. For his clients this was good news and this situation would only strengthen their negotiation power to buy the property.

He tried not to care, because becoming emotionally involved in the situation wouldn't be a sound decision for his own future well-being. But he couldn't stop himself from feeling regret that Kiki's plans were in jeopardy as he took his place down a line and began to pluck the black, inch-long insects from the stems and leaves of the many different blossoms and toss them into the buckets of soapy water.

Kiki worked alongside him, her easy chatter and upbeat mood making a tedious chore more enjoyable.

And as illogical as it was, he did care about her and her family.

The heat from the morning sun sent the beetles scurrying underground. Exhaustion weighed on Kiki's shoulders as she called a halt to the work.

Standing by the gate to hug and thank everyone as they filed out, she couldn't believe how touched she was by the hard work and dedication of each individual who'd stayed through the night picking bugs off the plants. Many said they'd be back that evening to complete the debugging. That went way beyond the call of duty.

As the last of the employees and their families left, Kiki went to where Ryan and Tutu were conversing on the porch stairs. It made no sense to her that Ryan would help. This insect infestation could ruin the farm. He should be champing at the bit to get their signatures on the documents he'd brought with him.

She wasn't sure what to make of him. He'd stayed calm and levelheaded yesterday when the fuel line had been cut, stranding them in the middle of nowhere. And she'd not only found herself really comfortable with him, but confiding in him about her jerk of an ex-boyfriend. She hadn't even told her family some of the details she'd shared with Ryan.

Allowing herself to be drawn to another main-lander wasn't a good idea. Granted, Ryan wasn't seeking a part of the Brill fortune, but he was after her heritage. She mustn't give in to any attraction or romantic nonsense. She and Ryan were like oil and water. And she was determined to have her way.

"Well done, Kiki, dear," Tutu said as Kiki stepped onto the porch.

"We've a long way to go yet," she replied, stretching the tight muscles of her back.

"True, but with so many people pitching in, it won't be long before we're rid of the little pests."

Tutu's confidence made Kiki smile. "You're right."

Tutu patted Kiki's arm. "If you two will excuse me, I'm going to bed. I think Pano should be back from his job in a few hours and he's not the most quiet of human's."

"Rest well," Ryan said as Tutu headed inside.

Left alone with Ryan, Kiki gave him her full attention. His once-pressed khaki pants and polo shirt now bore streaks of dirt amid wrinkles of wear. His dark hair had grooves from where he'd run his fingers through the silky-looking strands. Though he smiled, his eyes were weary.

Kiki's heart swelled with affection that she tried to fight. "Thank you, Ryan, for staying all night. That certainly wasn't necessary."

One dark eyebrow arched. "I think you needed every available set of hands you could find."

She acquiesced to that statement with a sheepish smile. "You're right. I'm grateful you stayed."

His grin jump-started her pulse. "Me, too. It was actually fun. I really enjoyed getting to know everyone. I've met some very good people on this island."

There was no way he could know how much his words meant to her. "This is a wonderful place to live." Though she did wish there wasn't the issue with the neighbors wanting her to sell her land so they could, also.

A shadow entered his gaze. "I've arranged to meet a security company here this afternoon to discuss what kinds of solutions they might have for Kaapa Flower Farm."

A boulder sank in the pit of her stomach. As much as she appreciated his concern and as much as they needed some type of security, she had no idea how the business could afford it. Every time she turned around, they were going deeper into a financial pit. "Wouldn't a dog be a good security measure?"

A dog she might be able to afford.

"It would be a start," Ryan replied, his expression thoughtful. "How about we run to the pound right now and see what they have?"

"Uh, well." She had so much to do. Just because the employees weren't here, didn't mean the farm could stop functioning. It was a business day. There were orders to fill, the specialty orchids in the green-house needed attention, plus the fertilizer truck needed to be replaced. Then there was Jeff Tolar who might want to kill her simply because her last name was Brill, and she really wanted to get out of the dirty clothes that were itching her skin. She was so not having a good week.

But if bringing home a dog would stave off having to spend money on a sophisticated security system, then that's what she had to do.

"Yes. That would be great. There's an animal shelter in Puunene."

They took his rented Mustang since hers was in the shop. The engine rumbled through the floorboard as Ryan drove like a man used to being in control. Kiki fought to stay awake, forcing herself to keep a vigilant eye in case they were followed while they zipped through Kihei and turned on the Mokuleie Highway passing fields of sugarcane.

When they reached the once-prosperous and now little more than a sugar mill town of Puunene, they stopped at the post office to ask directions to the animal shelter. The postal clerk's directions were easy to follow, and they arrived shortly at the large square building, which looked more like a warehouse than an animal shelter.

The property was surrounded by a chain-link fence. Several dogs were running and playing in the fenced-in yard. Kiki recognized two of the breeds.

One was a golden retriever and the other some sort of lab mix. She wasn't sure of the third dog's pedigree.

They entered the front door and were greeted by a woman from behind a long counter. She had graying hair cut in a bob to her pointed chin. Her green eyes, so bright in her pale face, were alight with interest. "Hello, there. I'm Vicki. What can I do for you today?"

"We're looking for a guard dog," Ryan replied.

Vicki nodded as if such a thing was an everyday request.

"And a companion for my Tutu," Kiki blurted impulsively.

"I have several you might be interested in. Just fill out this application." She reached into a drawer and pulled out a stapled packet. Sliding it across the counter, she said, "When you're done, we can talk about your needs. We are looking for loving, permanent homes for our animals and if the staff feels it necessary, we may need to do a home inspection."

"We won't be able to take the dog today?" Kiki asked.

Vicki shrugged. "That depends. Are there other dogs on the premises?"

"No," Kiki replied, looking at the daunting forms.

"Where do you two live?" Vicki asked.

"Near Kihei," Ryan responded.

Kiki stared at him. He hadn't corrected the

woman's assumption that they were a couple. An unsettled pleasure coursed through her.

"In an apartment or a house?" Vicki asked.

"Actually, on a farm. The Kaapa Flower Farm," Ryan stated.

Vicki beamed. "I know Lana Kaapa." She turned her green gaze on Kiki. "You must be her grand-daughter. She's talked so highly of you. I'm sure we'll be able to work something out. You just fill out those forms and then we can go see the doggies. In fact, I have one in mind I think will be perfect for you."

"Thank you," Kiki said, and sat down on a bench that ran along the windowed front. Ryan handed her a pen. She smiled and filled in the blank lines on the form as thoroughly and as quickly as she could.

She pulled out her checkbook and wrote out a check for the amount specified on the form. She didn't want to think about how little she had in her checking account. If things didn't change soon, she'd have to ask her parents for a loan.

And that was something she really didn't want to do, because there was no guarantee they would give her any money when she knew they'd rather see her and Tutu leave Maui, for good.

EIGHT

When Kiki was done, she handed the forms to Vicki.

"Come on back," she said, gesturing for them to follow her through a door that led to a large warehouse with dozens of kennels. Very few were occupied.

A good thing, Kiki guessed. They passed a small white fluffy poodle, a large mastiff that stuck its nose in the air as if testing their scent.

Vicki led them to a kennel where a medium-sized Australian shepherd lay dozing. As they approached, the black, tan and white dog rose to greet them, his hind end wagging and his lips stretched in a distinct semblance of a smile.

"This is Cody," Vicki announced.

"Oh, he's a handsome guy," Kiki exclaimed, her heart already falling for him.

"He just recently came to us. His family moved to California and didn't want the hassle of shipping him."

"How sad," Kiki said, and moved closer to the metal cage.

"How old is Cody?" Ryan asked.

"Three. He's a good boy. Very obedient. The nice thing about Aussies is they become very territorial, yet aren't vicious unless provoked." She opened the door. "Here, boy."

Cody trotted forward and immediately went to Kiki. She held out her hand for him to sniff, letting him become familiar with her before she tried to pet him. He licked her fingers. She laughed and then scrubbed him behind the ears.

"I like him," she stated, her gaze flying to Ryan. Her breath stalled at the expression on his face. She tried to quickly discern what she saw, affection, attraction, longing? He turned his attention away and left Kiki feeling a bit off-kilter.

"He seems like a good choice. Are his shots up-to-date?"

"Yes. He's good to go."

Kiki shifted her gaze to Vicki. "Do we have to wait twenty-four hours, like the forms said?"

Vicki smiled. "No. I know your grandmother, I know your farm. And you two seem like such a nice pair that I think Cody could go home with you today."

"We're just friends," Kiki corrected her, gesturing her hand between her and Ryan.

"Really.? I assumed… No matter." She waved her hand. "I'm sure Cody will be well taken care of. Let me get his leash and his records for you," she said, and hustled away.

Kiki bent down closer to Cody's snout. "Do you want to come home with me, Cody?"

"By the speed his backside is moving, I'd say that's a yes," Ryan remarked, drily.

Vicki came back with a thick collar with tags that she slipped around Cody's neck and then handed Kiki a black leash and a file folder full of papers. "Here's everything you need."

With her heart pounding, Kiki attached the leash to Cody's collar. She now owned a dog. She'd never had a pet before. Her parents had been too busy to agree to care for an animal.

Cody jumped right into the backseat of the Mustang without any coaxing.

"Looks as if he's anxious to leave here," Ryan said as he slipped into the driver's seat.

Fastening her seat belt, Kiki reached back to stroke Cody's soft fur. "Should we buckle him in?"

Ryan shook his head. "I don't think that would work." He glanced at Cody through the rearview mirror. "Cody, lie down."

Kiki clapped when Cody dropped to his belly, his head resting on his paws.

On the ride back to the farm they stopped at the pet store and bought food, two dishes—one for water and one for food. Kiki also bought a plush bed for her dog.

Her dog. Excitement made her antsy the rest of the drive home and she couldn't keep from smiling.

"You're pretty stoked, aren't you?" Ryan asked as he slowed the car to turn onto the Kaapa drive.

"Yes. I've never had a dog before. Have you?"

He shook his head. "Not one of my own. My mother had a little Bichon that drove me nuts as a kid. But when Lexie passed on, Mom never got another one. And I'm not home enough to own a pet," he said, bringing the car to a halt.

"That must be hard, to travel so much and never feel rooted," Kiki commented as she paused with her hand on the door. Her roots were here on the farm. The only place she felt she truly belonged.

"I've never thought of it that way. I guess my roots are in Boston with my family," he stated, and got out of the car.

Boston. Where he belonged. Kiki accepted that with a wry bit of sadness. She knew he'd leave eventually, had even tried to speed his departure, but over the past few days she'd grown to really enjoy having him so closely involved in her life. Of course, it was all just for one purpose, to work his way to securing her signature on the contract that would turn over the property. Not going to happen.

She climbed out and flipped the seat forward for Cody. He jumped out and began to sniff, running to and fro, his nose to the ground. He stopped to water a plant and then continued on his exploration of the farm. When he wandered too close to the driveway entrance, Kiki called him back. Cody came loping to her side.

"Good boy," she exclaimed. "Isn't he such a good boy?"

Ryan laughed. "Yes, he is. I'm going to leave you two to get to know each other. I'll be back at four to meet with the security company."

Kiki frowned. "But I have a dog now. I don't need anything else."

He stared at her, the determined expression on his handsome face unwavering. "The dog will help, but a security system is the best course of action."

She rebelled from saying she couldn't afford the cost, but how else would she make him understand that buying a security system wasn't a viable option? "Look, I do appreciate your persistence and your concern, but we can't. We can't afford the expense."

His lips curled upward slightly at the corners. "Let me worry about that."

"Let you worry about it," she said with a good dose of disbelief. Was he offering to buy the system? "You can't be serious."

He held up his hand, palm out. "At this point, Kiki, all I'm going to do is see what suggestions they have and see what can be negotiated. We won't commit to anything."

Not sure what to make of him or his actions, she said, "Fine. As along as we're agreed there's to be no deal made."

"Agreed."

The heartrending tenderness of his gaze sucked

the breath from her lungs. She fought the urge to reach out to touch him, to see if he were real or some figment of her imagination. What kind of man took such an interest in others when doing so went against his own interest? No man she'd ever met. She forced herself to speak past her confusion. "Then I guess we'll see you at four."

With a smile and a salute, Ryan sauntered to his car, leaving Kiki wondering why tears clogged her throat and burned at the back of her eyes.

Twilight descended with a cooling trade wind that rustled through the fronds of the hillside palms and whipped Ryan's hair in a frenzied dance. He smoothed back a chuck of hair from in front of his eyes as he bent to pluck more beetles from exotic plants he'd never seen before in his life. Spiky, tubular ones, others with thorny tips and still others that looked like feathers from a bird. The different scents filled his nostrils until he could no longer smell anything.

Around him many of the workers from the night before had returned along with newer faces, filling the rows around him.

The stress of the last few days was taking its toll on Kiki, if the tight lines around her mouth and the dark circles under her eyes were any indication. Concern for her well-being throbbed in his head and his heart.

She couldn't keep pushing herself like this or she'd collapse. Not something Ryan intended to let happen. She needed rest. And he guessed she hadn't rested while he'd been at his own condo trying to sleep.

When he'd arrived back on the farm to meet the security company, Kiki had been working in the greenhouse, Cody at her heels. She hadn't changed clothes nor had she eaten. That had sent his blood pressure soaring, but he'd refrained from lecturing her. She didn't need a parent. She needed support.

After discussing the possible solutions for securing the farm's property and asking for a quote on a plan he'd submitted, Ryan made dinner for Kiki and Tutu before they resumed their work in the field.

One other surprising newcomer was Nik. Apparently he had the night off and offered his services. He seemed to be making a point of sticking close to Kiki, which irrationally, left Ryan in a foul mood. Who better to keep her safe, after all.

Ryan left the plant he'd been working on and approached Nik. "So, Officer, any word on that jar? Fingerprints or something?" Ryan asked, standing beside Nik and Kiki at one of the soapy buckets of water.

"There weren't fingerprints. Whoever let the bugs go probably wore gloves," Nik responded, his dark eyes catching a flash of light. "But the only way anyone could get this kind of quantity would be to import the bugs from Japan. We're in contact with customs, working to trace the path the beetles have taken. We're hoping that path will lead us to the culprit."

"Too bad there's no easy way to find the jerk who did this," Ryan said as he stepped around Nik to be closer to Kiki. He took the bag of squirming bugs from her hand to dump them in the bucket.

She gave him a tired smile. "Thank you."

"You know, Kiki, you should really consider how hard all of this is on Tutu," Nik said, his voice low and his tone hard.

Kiki flinched. "I am."

Anger flaring hot in Ryan, he whipped his gaze to Nik. "She's well aware of the strain this is putting on Tutu."

Nik's gaze narrowed.

Tears swam in Kiki's eyes. "I've repeatedly asked her to stop and go rest, but she won't listen."

"You know, if you just sold this place your grandmother would be able to rest and have a comfortable life from here on out," Nik stated.

Kiki gave a dry laugh. "You sound like Pano."

Nik shrugged his big shoulders. "We all want what's best for both you and Tutu."

Ryan wanted to say Nik should stay out of it, that it wasn't any of his business. But Nik was a family friend and he was only repeating what Ryan himself had said only a few days before.

"And you don't think I do? Don't you think I want

Tutu to be comfortable? But this is her home. I have to save her home."

Even in the shadowed light of the moon, Nik's expression showed doubt. "Right."

Kiki turned away. "Let's get back to work."

Ryan wanted to reach out to Kiki, to offer her his support, his comfort and tell her how much he admired her determination and drive, but it was exactly those traits that were keeping him from successfully acquiring the Kaapa property.

Somehow over the last few days he'd lost his momentum, his fire to close the deal. He'd never been in such a quandary before.

How would he earn the bonus promised him if he really didn't want to see the Kaapa Flower Farm fail?

"I want to thank you all for your hard work. I can't express how much this means to Tutu and me."

Kiki stood on the porch addressing the workers who'd stayed through another night of removing the Japanese beetles from the flower crop. Fatigue etched lines in every face that stared back at her. They were all exhausted as the humidity rose along with the morning sun.

"I won't ask for any of you to come back tonight. I'm pretty sure we were successful in getting rid of the majority of insects. We'll be taking other measures to kill off any strays. So go home, rest, and those who are employed here, we'll see back tomorrow morning."

The crowd dispersed and soon the only people left were Tutu, Nik and Ryan. Pano hadn't shown up last night and still hadn't returned this morning, even though his stuff was strewn about the room he was sleeping in. She guessed his job for the state transportation department took precedence over their family crisis. She shouldn't feel hurt or resentful and told herself she was being ridiculous. Of course he had to go to his job.

As she came to stand beside her grandmother, Nik was saying, "Just think about it, Tutu."

"Think about what?" Kiki asked, though she had a good suspicion that Nik and Ryan had joined forces to coerce her grandmother into selling. Anger, hot and potent, flushed through her. She wouldn't have been surprised if Ryan had been the one talking to Tutu about selling, that was his sole purpose here. But Nik? Was everyone convinced she would fail?

Tutu took Kiki's hand. "I was telling Ryan I haven't had a chance to look over the documents, but that we would this afternoon and have an answer for him tomorrow."

Kiki swallowed back the harsh words that sprang to her lips. Reigning in her upset, she said, "Fine. Tomorrow, then. Goodbye."

Tutu squeezed her hand in silent admonishment, but Kiki didn't regret her rude dismissal. The men were trying to undermine her hold on the farm, trying to convince her grandmother that selling the land would be a good thing.

But how could they still not realize that without the Kaapa Flower Farm, Kiki would have nowhere to belong.

The headlights of the rented Mustang cut across the Kaapa fields as Ryan turned on to the driveway. His mouth tightened in exasperation as he caught a glimpse of Kiki in the middle of a grouping of bird-of-paradise flowers, some of their long stalks nearly reaching her shoulder. More than likely checking the plants again for the pests. The woman never gave up.

She'd work herself until she dropped. Though an admirable trait, Ryan couldn't help but feel the need to relieve her of her burdens. Or at the very least help her take some downtime.

He'd been sitting on the deck of his condo, watching the setting sun dip low over the water, the oranges and reds painting the sky in bold streaks, when Horatio called demanding to know when they'd have an answer.

Tomorrow. Horatio would have to be satisfied with waiting until then. But Ryan couldn't stop the thoughts of Kiki and all the strange events from occupying his mind.

Someone was going to great lengths to bring about the ruin of the farm. Was it someone who wanted the property sold? Or was it the ex-con that was stalking her grandfather, the judge?

Ryan had called Nik to assure himself that the authorities were aware of the situation. Nik guaranteed him that if the ex-con, a man named Jeff Tolar, was to step foot on the island he'd be immediately picked up.

But still. What if the man used an alias and a disguise?

Unable to sit idle, knowing that Kiki wouldn't be resting, he'd driven back to the farm. And sure enough, there she was, back in the field.

He parked and climbed out from behind the wheel. Cody came loping over, looking for attention. "Hi, boy."

Ryan scratched him behind the ear before heading toward where she stood staring at him, her long hair loose about her shoulders, her beautiful face bathed in the rising moon's light.

"What are you doing here?" she asked as he stopped a few feet from her. In her hands she held a bucket of sudsy water and a plastic bag.

"Have you found any more?"

She shook her head. "Not yet."

He stepped closer and took the bucket and bag from her hands and set them on the ground before capturing her hand in his. "Come with me for a walk on the beach."

"I can't. I need to be sure."

"You were sure this morning. Come on, let's take Cody and go for a walk. You need some downtime."

She pulled her hand away. "Look, you'll get your answer tomorrow. Come back then."

"This isn't about the sale," he stated, knowing in his heart his words were true.

She cocked her head to the side. "Then what's this about?"

He wasn't sure himself so he stayed focused on his earlier proclamation. "It's about taking some time to relax. About taking a break from your worries. Come with me. I'll bring you back in an hour."

"I don't know," she started to say.

He pressed a finger to her soft lips. "Don't think about it. Just come with me. I promise, no talk of the farm or selling."

She nodded and he dropped his hand, though warmth from her touch lingered on his skin.

"Let me go tell Tutu."

He stepped aside so she could pass. Her scent, fresh like a crisp apple, wrapped around his senses. He moved to wait by the car with Cody at his heels.

When she returned, she was carrying a basket and a blanket. He arched an eyebrow as she set them on the backseat next to Cody. "What do we have here?"

"Tutu insisted," she said as she slid into the passenger seat. "Some cheese, crackers and sodas."

"Nice. A picnic on the beach. I like it," he replied as he maneuvered the car out of the driveway and headed toward the beach.

At Kiki's direction, he parked in a public parking

lot. Ryan grabbed a flashlight from the glove box and followed Kiki and Cody down the road until they came to a path between two houses that led to a small cove, illuminated by the porch lights of the two houses.

"Is this okay?" Ryan asked, wondering how the occupants would feel about intruders on their beach.

Spreading out the blanket over the soft sand, she replied, "It's fine. I know both the owners. They aren't in residence right now."

For the next hour they talked about life, sports, the theater and anything else that came to mind that didn't pertain to their work. They shared laughter as they watched Cody exploring the cove, digging at the sand when he found the air bubbles of a sand crab.

Ryan and Kiki ate some of their snack and then walked down to the water's edge. The balmy night swirled around them, the sounds of the churning ocean relaxing, while the glow of the moon provided enough light to see the contented expression in Kiki's eyes.

Ryan couldn't remember ever feeling so comfortable or relaxed with another person. It was as if, for this moment in time, the rest of the world didn't exist.

Slipping his arm around Kiki felt natural as in the distance they watched a cruise ship sail over the ocean. The lights of the vessel like a thousand tiny diamonds in the night.

"Thank you, Ryan," Kiki whispered. "I really needed this."

"My pleasure," he replied, enjoying the feel of her close to his side.

She made a little noise, one that sounded suspiciously like a scoff.

He tilted her face up with his hand. "Really, Kiki. I've never felt so comfortable or relaxed with anyone as I do you."

The high moon shone in her warm eyes. "Right. You, Mr. Charmer? I'm sure you've broken hearts everywhere you go."

He frowned, not happy she had such a low opinion of him. "No. I don't do involved. Usually."

"Usually?"

"The last couple of days, being here on the island and working with you…I don't know how to explain it."

"Are you going to break my heart, Ryan?"

Purposely misunderstanding her comment, his mouth quirked. "I thought we weren't going to talk business."

"I'm not talking business. I talking about you and me."

He was afraid of that. Them together as a couple scared him spitless. He couldn't come up with any logical way for that to happen. Remaining silent and letting others talk had always been a tactic he used with clients. One he chose to employ now with Kiki.

"The last few days," she continued, stoking the

tension between them. "Like you said, working together, sharing the burden. And here, tonight. Is this all some game? Some ploy, a means to an end?"

Touched by the vulnerability in her voice, he smoothed back her hair from the side of her face. "Man, that guy did a number on you." He hated that her sense of trust had been destroyed. "Here, tonight, Kiki, there are no hidden agendas." He traced the curve of her cheekbone with his fingertips. "I enjoy being with you."

She turned her face into his palm. "I enjoy being with you, too."

He slid his hand through her hair and pulled her closer with the arm that held her tight. Her breathing accelerated. He dipped his head. Her eyes widened. He hovered, waiting for encouragement or refusal. She arched forward, closing the distance between them, pressing her lips against his. Her kiss was so sweet, so perfect.

Yearning exploded behind his closed eyelids. The kiss deepened. Her arms wrapped around him. Powerful emotions surged in his chest, all the affection and attraction for her he'd been conscious of came to life as he took her willing mouth.

A low rumble vibrated through the air. The noise registered as a warning from Cody just as the dog's growl turned to a fierce bark.

NINE

Ryan broke the kiss as adrenaline-fueled panic pumped through his blood. He turned to see Cody snarling and barking at the bushes.

Kiki's grip tightened. "Someone's there." Stark terror rang in her voice.

Releasing her, Ryan ran from where they stood at the water's edge back to the blanket, grabbed the flashlight and shone it on the bushes running along the fence of the house where Cody continued to bark and jump as if trying to get to someone on the other side.

Ryan moved closer, shining the light on the sandy ground around the shrubs. There were footprints. With the light he followed the trail along the path to the parking lot.

Kiki calmed Cody down. "It's okay, boy. They're gone now."

Ryan came back. "I think whoever it was, came in from the path and then went over the fence when Cody noticed him."

Kiki shivered, wrapping her arms around her middle. "Someone was spying on us?"

Creeped out and wanting to get Kiki back to safety, Ryan said, "I don't know. But let's pack up and get out of here."

They hurried with the blanket and basket back to his car. He halted Kiki with his hand before he cautiously approached, looking for any signs of tampering. He opened the car door and started the engine before he allowed Kiki and Cody to climb in. Thinking of Tutu, he sped back toward the farm.

When they arrived, Kiki refused to wait in the car, but jumped out and raced up the porch stairs.

Ryan caught up to her and dragged her behind him. "Let me go first," he instructed.

He opened the door, Cody bolted in, but when he didn't make any sound, Ryan, with Kiki at his back, stepped inside. Tutu was sitting on the couch watching television. Cody sat at her feet. Tutu cooed to the dog before smiling a welcome to Ryan and Kiki.

Ryan let out a relieved breath, gave Tutu a wave and motioned Kiki back outside.

"I'm going to call Nik and tell him about someone watching us," he said as he pulled out his cell phone.

Kiki nodded, her expression pensive.

Nik promised Ryan he'd make sure the patrols already driving by the Kaapas were extra alert, but that's all he could do for the moment.

Pressing the end button and tucking his phone

back into his pocket, Ryan ran a hand through his hair. "I don't like leaving you two here alone. Where's Pano?"

She shrugged. "I don't know. He'll turn up."

"When you go back into the house, make sure all the doors and windows are locked, okay?"

"I will."

He should say good-night and leave, but he didn't want to. He wanted to resume the kiss that had ended way too soon.

She stared at him, her eyes full of questions.

Questions he wasn't prepared to answer. His emotions were muddled, which never made for good business. And he was all about business. Wasn't he?

"Ryan?"

"Yes?"

"About what happened on the beach—"

He pressed a finger to her lips to stop her from saying it was a mistake. He didn't want to hear her say the words, didn't want to believe them. How could something that felt so right be a mistake?

Leaning closer, he replaced his finger on her mouth with his lips. A sweet chaste kiss that made him ache deep in his soul in a way he'd never experienced. Attraction flared, yes, but it was more than just a physical response. He felt more. Deep inside where he didn't realize he could feel. Unnerved, he stepped back. "Good night, Kiki. Until tomorrow."

Tomorrow. So much hinged on the results of the

next day. And he wasn't sure which way he hoped the resolution would go. He wanted his money from procuring Kiki's and Tutu's signatures on the contract, but yet, he didn't want to see the Kaapa Flower Farm dissolved, because he knew what that would mean to Kiki.

Every choice in his life had been driven by the need to secure his financial future. He'd never wavered from that goal, until now.

Until a certain exotic beauty entered his life, making him care in ways he never had before.

But caring for Kiki wouldn't secure Ryan's future.

Kiki watched the red taillights of Ryan's car disappear into the night. She sighed with a mixture of longing and regret.

Tomorrow everything would change between them once she gave him her and Tutu's answer. An answer they as of yet hadn't come to agreement on. The first offer had been staggering at ten million and even more so now at fifteen million. Tutu kept waffling and Kiki wasn't going to budge. She did not want to give up on the farm. No matter how badly someone out there wanted to force her to quit.

She turned to head inside when a movement in her peripheral vision grabbed her attention. From inside the house Cody barked.

A scream built in Kiki's chest as she turned fully to face the threat. A man came out of the shadow of the house and stepped into the porch light. The curtain at the window drew back and Tutu peered out. She smiled when she saw her grandchildren. Cody stopped barking.

"Pano," she breathed out, her heart beating in her throat. "You scared me. What are you doing?"

"Watching you make nice with the Haole," he said with a sneer as he came up the stairs.

Kiki wrinkled her nose at the stench of alcohol and tobacco emanating off him in waves. "You've been out partying. Shouldn't you be at work?"

He laughed, a caustic sound that stirred the humid night air. "You worried about me, cousin?" he asked, leaning in.

Not liking the way he crowded her, she stepped to the door, her hand on the knob. "You better sober up before Tutu sees you like this."

"You gonna rat me out?"

"No. But you know it will break her heart to see you so…" She waved a hand at him to indicate his condition.

His clothes were mussed as if he'd worn them for too long. In fact, come to think of it, he was wearing the same cargo pants and T-shirt he'd left the house in on Sunday. Two days ago. She narrowed her gaze at him. "Where have you been for the past two days?"

He shrugged. "Around. What's it to you?"

Having had enough experience dealing with him as a drunk teen, she knew by his belligerent tone that talking to him while he was in this condition wouldn't do any good. Instead she said, "Come inside and sleep it off."

"What about Tutu?" he said, swaying slightly.

She took him firmly by the arm. "We'll tell her you don't feel well."

He nodded. "I don't. I think I'm going to be sick."

She directed him to the edge of the porch. He leaned over the railing and threw up. Kiki turned away.

Pano straightened. "Sorry about that."

"Yeah, yeah." She maneuvered him inside the house. Cody came running and skidded to a halt with his teeth bared. "It's okay, boy," she soothed.

"What's that thing?" Pano accused.

"My dog, Cody."

Pano grunted and nearly tripped over his own feet.

Thankfully, Tutu wasn't in the living room. Kiki steered Pano down the hall to the room he currently occupied and helped him to settle back on the twin-size bed.

"Do you want me to call your boss and tell him you're sick."

He shook his head and closed his eyes with a groan.

"Good night, Pano," she said, and turned off the light.

Just as she was closing the door, he said, "Thank you, Kiki."

"You're welcome," she whispered, feeling as though they'd been transported back to when they were teenagers. Pano was always doing crazy stunts and getting himself in trouble. Kiki had covered for him when she could.

Now that they were adults she'd thought those days were long gone. Not so much.

Once in her own room with Cody curled up at the foot of her bed, she picked up the phone to call her parents.

Her father answered on the second ring. "Kiki, are you all right?"

"Yes. Sorry to wake you."

"You didn't. We've only been home a short time. We were at the annual children's hospital fund-raiser."

Leaning back against the wall, Kiki could picture her parents in their black-tie attire. Dad would wear his usual black classic tux. Kiki wondered what dress her mother chose for the night. The red Versace or the lavender Vera Wang? Or maybe something new that Kiki hadn't seen. Whatever her mother wore, she'd be striking. "Did you have a good time?"

"Yes. It was a successful event. Have there been any more incidents there?"

Kiki hesitated. She really didn't want to worry them, yet she knew if they found out she was holding back information, they'd be livid and hurt. "A few strange things. But Nik has a patrol car coming by, and I bought a dog. He's the most beautiful guy. His name's Cody and he's an Australian shepherd."

"A dog is a good idea. Now what strange things?"

"Someone let loose a bunch of Japanese beetles in the crop. Not the work of Grandfather's stalker, I'm sure."

"No, I don't suppose so." His voice took on a pensive note.

The urge to ask for help flooded her mouth, but she choked back the words. She wouldn't ask. Not yet. Not unless the situation became dire. But deep inside it hurt that her father didn't offer any assistance. Her mouth twisted ruefully. He rarely did, believing that the only way one succeeded in life was through hard work, not handouts.

The pause before he spoke raised the hairs on Kiki's nape.

"No one has been hurt."

"But something has happened?" Kiki held her breath.

"Your grandmother is sure that someone broke into the house. But the police didn't find any evidence confirming her suspicion. Your grandparents are sequestered in their Maine house for now."

Kiki had never visited the retirement residence her grandparents bought on the coast of Maine. "Do they have protection there?"

"Yes. They are well taken care of there."

"So has Grandfather retired?"

"Yes. It will be official come the first of the year. I'm going to let you go now, dear. We miss you."

"You could come visit?" Kiki suggested for the millionth time.

"Maybe when things settle down."

"Okay. Tell Mom I love her."

"Will do. Good night."

Her father hung up. Kiki replaced the receiver and snuggled down under the covers.

She closed her eyes and cleared her mind as she spoke to God.

"Lord, please protect my grandparents and my parents. And all the Brills. I pray for Tutu, that You'd give her wisdom and help us to make the right decision tomorrow. And, Lord, bless Ryan. He really is a good man."

A man she had no business getting involved with. She was only putting her heart at risk again. His life was back in Boston. Hers was here.

There was no middle ground.

Ryan sipped his morning coffee out on the lanai overlooking the pool, the well-tended lawn and Keawakapu Beach. No clouds dotted the powder-blue sky, and the sun's warming rays were cooled slightly by a mild trade wind. On the horizon, boats with white sails lazily toured the Pacific Ocean. Another glorious day in paradise.

Only, for Ryan it was already a tense day. Today

the Kaapas would make a decision. And Ryan was pretty sure what that decision would be. There was no way Kiki would give up the flower farm, and Tutu would want Kiki to be happy.

Ryan scrubbed a hand over his jaw. He hadn't given his all to this project; he hadn't pushed the issue with Kiki and Tutu. There had simply been so many other more immediate concerns for the Kaapa women that throwing a sales pitch at them had seemed wrong. He'd crossed the line of professionalism and let Kiki's strength of character and her loving and generous nature get under his skin.

Bad judgment call. All he'd wanted was to secure her signature on the contract and then leave paradise.

From now on he'd keep the relationship professional; he wasn't staying and she would never leave her island home.

He glanced at his watch, only two more hours until he was expected at the farm to receive their answer.

A knock on the condo door brought him to his feet. Setting his mug on the metal table, he walked past the blue-and-yellow-patterned upholstered couch, bamboo coffee table and small square eating table and two chairs on his way to the door. There was no peephole, so when he opened the door, he wasn't prepared to find Horatio Lewis on his doorstep.

"This is a surprise," Ryan said.

"Why haven't you secured this deal?" In his mid-sixties with sparse salt-and-pepper hair and blue eyes behind thick glasses, Horatio stood six feet four inches tall, and he tried to use every inch of that height to intimidate anyone who stood in his way.

Ryan didn't intimidate easily. Gesturing with his hand for Horatio to enter, Ryan said, "I told you I'd have an answer this afternoon. When did you get to the island?"

Horatio stopped in the middle of the cramped condo and perused the place with a critical expression. "This is so provincial."

Ryan felt heat rise in his cheeks; he'd had the same thought when he'd first walked in. But the simplicity of the condo and the slow pace of the island life had grown on him.

"Care for coffee?" Ryan asked as he moved to the kitchenette, deliberately ignoring his question.

Horatio waved away the offer. "I want to know where we stand on this deal. You should have had this sewn up long before now."

"The Kaapa Farm has run into some problems over the last few days. Mrs. Kaapa and Ms. Brill have been a bit preoccupied," Ryan replied, thinking *preoccupied* was an understatement.

"Problems are good for us," Horatio stated. "Do you think they'll sell?"

"I've given them the offer. They have promised to give me an answer today. But I told you this on the phone last night. Why didn't you tell me you were on the island?"

"What does it matter? I'll go with you today to seal this deal. We won't take no for answer," Horatio stated, his eyes determined behind his glasses.

Ryan didn't want Horatio to come with him, didn't want the man pressuring the women. They'd been through enough the last few days. They shouldn't have to deal with Horatio Lewis. Especially since Ryan was almost certain their answer was going to be no, they wouldn't sell. Who knew how Horatio would react to that news.

Ryan picked up his car keys and wallet. "Hey, since you're here, let's take a drive."

"I don't want to go sightseeing," Horatio groused.

Ryan wasn't going to take no for an answer. "Come on, I want to show you some other properties that might be of interest."

Horatio narrowed his gaze. "You setting me up, boy? You gonna take the Kaapa properties for yourself?"

Ryan's chin dipped as he stared through lowered brows at the man. "Now, why would I do that. I only get my money if you find a place for your investors to build their resort."

"True. But the Kaapa land is the best choice."

"But not the only choice," Ryan insisted, and steered Horatio out of the condo.

Thanks to Kiki, Ryan did have other options to

present. If he could convince Horatio, and in turn, the investors, to rethink the layout and design of the resort, the first of the two pieces of property Kiki had shown him would be viable. Ryan just might manage to save Kiki's farm *and* collect the money promised to him.

TEN

Kiki wiped the perspiration from her brow with her forearm. The greenhouse grew more humid as morning stretched into noontime. Around her, dozens of exotic orchids grew in a splendid display of color, from lavender to hot pink and every shade in between. She lovingly tended to each plant. Many of the unique blossoms were hybrids of plants her grandfather had originally seeded. These were her babies now. Her prizes.

Her gaze strayed to the clock. Ryan would be arriving soon for his answer. He wasn't going to be happy. Maybe she should bring Ryan into the greenhouse. Then maybe he'd have a better understanding of why she couldn't give up the farm.

Though the commercial crop of flowers were the business's financial mainstay, these exceptional and striking plants were what made all the hard work of keeping the farm alive worth it. The legacy of her grandfather's family was in each and every plant.

A commotion outside drew her attention. What now?

Cody rose and let out one bark before going to the door to be let out.

Setting aside the trowel and the sugar-rich, sterile agar that she'd been using to start a crop of new seedlings, she walked out of the four-sided glass greenhouse. Cooling air dried some of the moisture on her skin. She headed to where a group of employees were arguing.

"You go tell her," insisted Sue Kim, one of the women who prepared the harvested plants for distribution.

"Shh. Here she comes." Flo Chen, another woman who helped with the prework, shushed the other woman.

Kiki halted as the eight people shifted to face her. Dread sank to the pit of her stomach as she realized that the three deliverymen, who should have already been en route with their deliveries were part of the group. "Tell me what?"

For a moment they were all silent, then Phil, an older man who had come to the island as a boy from Guam, said, "Someone slashed the tires on the delivery trucks."

Shock stole her breath. Blood pounded in her ears. "On all of them?" she managed to ask.

Phil nodded to confirm.

Slashed tires. On all three delivery trucks. Each

truck had eight tires. How on earth could the farm afford to buy new tires along with a new fertilizer truck? They had insurance, which would help, though after reporting the pipe bomb, the beetles and now this, she could just guess her premiums were going to skyrocket.

But having insurance didn't solve the problem right now. Right now she had to figure out how to get the orders to the buyers. "Pickup trucks. We need to find a bunch of pickups to get today's orders out."

"Good idea," said Phil. "We'll start asking around."

The group dispersed and Kiki ran to the house to call the insurance agent. Before she reached the porch, she heard her name being called. A young man named Edgar came running from the fields.

He came to a puffing halt next to her. "The water. The water's not working."

Her mind blowing, she said, "What do you mean, not working?"

"The valve turns but no water comes out."

She sank to the bottom stair of the porch. Great. Had she forgotten to pay the water bill? But her gut told her a lapsed bill wasn't the problem. Someone, somehow had cut the water.

"Miss Kiki, you okay?"

Remembering the scripture from the previous Sunday's sermon, she repeated the words in her head,

Be strong and of good courage. Be strong and of good courage. Taking strength from the verse, she rose. "Yes, Edgar. I'll take care of it."

The young man nodded and trotted back toward the field.

She was not going to let anyone force her to sell no matter how badly they damaged the equipment. She wouldn't give in.

Her legacy was at stake.

As Ryan, with Horatio in the passenger seat, drove into the driveway of the Kaapa Flower Farm, Ryan's gut twisted with apprehension. Nik's police car was parked near the house, along with several others. In the far corner of the field several uniformed officers seemed to be gathering evidence. Ryan had a moment of déjà vu going back to the day when the fertilizer truck exploded.

Had something happened to Kiki?

"This is just as I remembered it," Horatio commented from the passenger seat. "We are definetly not taking no for an answer."

Heart pounding, Ryan brought the car to a halt and jumped out without replying. He couldn't think about the deal right now, he had to find Kiki and make sure she and Tutu were okay. He should have insisted that the security system be put in place when the company came out. Instead he'd allowed Kiki to put off the installation.

He found Kiki, Tutu and Nik behind the green-house. Cody came over to nuzzle his leg.

"What's happened?" Ryan went directly to Kiki and slid an arm around her shoulders, regardless that he'd already told himself to stay professional toward her. He could feel Horatio's stare, but he chose to ignore anything but Kiki. He didn't feel very professional at the moment, only protective. "You okay?"

She looked physically okay, aside from her exhaustion, but the despair in her gaze tore at his insides.

She sighed before answering. "Just more of the same. Someone out to force my hand."

Ryan looked to Nik who nodded. "Vandalism." He pointed to the three delivery trucks. "Slashed tires and a damaged water pipe."

Ryan's jaw tightened and his gaze jerked to where he could see Horatio, who now stood near the field surveying the land. Did he have something to do with this? He was here on the island when he shouldn't be. Distrust slithered down Ryan's spine.

"Cody didn't alert you?" Ryan asked, looking over to the dog, who had gone to lie in the shade.

Kiki shook her. "No. Nothing."

So much for a guard dog.

"What can be done?" Ryan asked, hoping there was some quick way to remedy this latest bit of sabotage.

"We managed to get today's deliveries out the

door by borrowing several pickup trucks," Kiki stated, her voice hard.

Tutu said, "But the guy from the Department of Water Supply says it will take a few days to get the pipe repaired and the water flowing again." The anxiety in her dark eyes reached out to Ryan.

Without water, even for a day, they could lose all the plants. "What about the house?"

"We're without water there, too," Kiki stated.

Ryan clenched his free hand. "We'll get you ladies into a hotel until this is resolved. In the meantime, there has to be a way to get water to the crops."

"There is," Kiki said. She met his gaze, her eyes bleak. "We could ask the neighbors if we can divert some of their water to us. But considering one of them is probably behind this, I doubt they'll oblige."

Ryan hated seeing the defeat in her eyes. "I'll go talk to them," he offered.

She smiled her thanks and leaned against him for a moment. "Thank you."

"Kiki, there is no evidence to support your suspicion that the neighbors are involved. And I think it would be better if I make the approach," Nik stated, his gaze settling on Ryan.

Not sure what to make of the hint of challenge in Nik's gaze, Ryan shrugged. "Didn't mean to usurp your authority. If you think they'll cooperate better for you, then by all means, you ask."

Nik nodded, the tension in his gaze lessening. "I'll

go take care of that now. The techs will finish up with their investigation soon and be out of your way," he said, and turned to leave.

"Officer," Horatio greeted Nik as they passed.

Horatio raised an eyebrow at Ryan as he joined them. Feeling uncomfortable with his display of affection toward Kiki, Ryan dropped his arm while he made the introductions.

"Ladies." Horatio straightened the cuff of his finely woven pale yellow dress shirt. He looked very out of place with his shiny black shoes and black trousers. Much like Ryan must have looked when he'd first approached Kiki.

"Ryan tells me you are ready to make a decision." Horatio peered at each woman as if searching for the crack in the armor. "I hope you agree that the offer Ryan presented to you is beyond fair for the purchase of your land."

Tutu stepped forward, her usually warm brown eyes drilling Horatio. "Mr. Lewis, I apologize, but at the moment we're in the middle of a crisis."

"Obviously. And though my timing seems a bit awkward, I believe now may be the exact time to come to terms," Horatio replied, his smile oozing charm.

Ryan gritted his teeth, wanting to drag Horatio away by the scruff of the neck. "We can reschedule this conversation."

Horatio's eyes behind the lenses of his glasses

grew hard as he sliced a look at Ryan before continuing to speak. "What is keeping you from selling? The farm is obviously struggling. Selling would relieve you of the burden. We do have negotiating room on the price."

Ryan stared. What? Since when? Irritation simmered low in his gut.

Kiki stepped forward, her spine straight and her chin held high. "We are not selling. Not now or anytime in the near future. Now, if you two will excuse us—" Kiki took her grandmother's arm "—we have much to do." The two women started to walk away.

Horatio blocked their path. "But think of all you could do with the money we've offered. The life you could live."

By the disdain on Kiki's face it was obvious she wasn't buying into that rationale. Neither was Ryan. Not now that he'd been a part of Kiki's life.

Beads of sweat broke out on Horatio's high brow. "Think of what could be done with this land. A beautiful resort, providing jobs for hundreds of locals, not to mention the fortune in tourism that would be passed along to many others."

Ryan had to hand it to Horatio for playing the greater good guilt card. But Kiki just shook her head and stepped around him.

"I'm staying at the Fairmont if you change your mind. I'll be here until Sunday morning. That gives you three days to change your mind," Horatio called after the women.

Kiki waved her hand to indicate she heard as she led her grandmother to the house. Just before she disappeared inside, she turned to meet Ryan's gaze.

Wishing he could stay with her and keep the world at bay for her, he mouthed, "I'm sorry."

She gave a slight nod and disappeared inside.

"Well, you blew that," Horatio stormed. "Why didn't you go for the kill? You're supposed to be this hotshot deal closer and yet you let them say no."

Seething with anger, Ryan growled, "Come on, we're leaving."

Not waiting for Horatio, Ryan stalked back to the car. He couldn't shake the notion that Horatio had something to do with all the vandalism. Ryan had heard rumors in the past about Horatio's less-than-ethical business practices and had even cautioned the man that Ryan wouldn't tolerate any shadiness. And this went beyond shady. This was intolerable.

Horatio climbed into the passenger seat. "Do you think there's a chance they'll change their minds?"

"No," Ryan said succinctly as he headed them back toward Horatio's hotel. "Tell me the truth, Horatio. Are you behind the vandalism on the Kaapa Farm?"

"What? Of course not."

Ryan slanted the man a probing glance. Horatio's face gave nothing away. Was he telling the truth? Or was he just a good liar?

Since Ryan had no proof of wrongdoing by Horatio, he wouldn't officially accuse him. But he would never trust the man again.

"What's up with you and that girl?" Horatio asked, his voice tight.

The word *nothing* sprang to Ryan's lips, but he swallowed the word because saying so would be a lie.

He cared for her, enjoyed being with her and couldn't stand to see her hurting. But because he didn't trust Horatio, all Ryan would reveal was, "We've become friends."

Horatio scoffed. "Nothing worse than getting emotionally involved with the client. You, of all people, should know that. It taints your objectivity. Which it clearly has here. I'm telling you, Ryan, if I don't leave Maui with a signed contract, you will not be seeing a penny."

Clamping his jaw tight, Ryan allowed a tense silence to permeate the conversation as he drove. Finally, Ryan brought the Mustang to a halt under the wide marble-arched breezeway of the Fairmont Hotel.

For a moment he stared straight ahead, not really seeing the picturesque landscape or the crystalline blue waters of the Pacific Ocean. Instead he saw Kiki's face, the defeat in her eyes, and his heart twisted in misery on her behalf. She shouldn't have to be forced into this position. It wasn't fair. It wasn't honorable.

Ryan was at a crossroads in his life. He could choose to dance to Horatio's tune or he could follow his heart. Something he'd never done before. Instead, always relying on logic and what made the best business sense to direct his life. Kiki had managed to breach the barricades he'd erected around his heart.

There was only one path he could take.

He turned to fully face Horatio. "The deal is off. Completely. You leave the Kaapa women alone. They are not selling."

"You can't be serious." Horatio's shocked tone reverberated within the interior of the car.

Feeling confident and right about his decision, Ryan said succinctly, "Dead serious."

A muscle in Horatio's jaw ticked. "You'll come to regret this."

Ryan stiffened. "Are you threatening me?"

Horatio jerked the door opened. "I'm saying that once word gets out that you've backed out on a client, you'll never find work again."

The pronouncement hit Ryan like a left hook to the gut. But even knowing that he was jeopardizing his career didn't make him want to change his mind.

"I'll take my chances," Ryan replied, his voice cold and hard even to his own ears.

Horatio slammed the car door like a petulant child and stalked away. Ryan was glad to be rid of him. He drove away from the Fairmont and pulled into a public parking lot up the road. His hands shook when he lifted them off the steering wheel. He took deep breaths to calm his nerves. He'd just walked away from a small fortune, not to mention that he now couldn't expense the condo or the car to the Lewis Corp.

And he had no doubt Horatio would make good his threat to besmirch Ryan's reputation. But none of that mattered.

His brother Brody had only this past summer lectured Ryan on his driving need to accumulate wealth versus finding and sustaining relationships with people. Yeah, easy for Brody to talk. His brother had a great wife in Kate. And Patrick, too, had found someone he'd willingly given up his identity for.

But they didn't understand what it was like to be the youngest; they weren't the ones who always had to make do with hand-me-downs when they couldn't afford anything else.

His brothers didn't understand how much having financial security meant to Ryan.

But he still couldn't force Kiki into selling.

The realization rocked him to the core. He refused to analyze why. It was a fact and that was that. He needed to get his head on straight, get back on track and leave the island.

But first he had to make sure Kiki was protected.

ELEVEN

Kiki watched through the front-room window as Ryan's car came up the driveway. Why was he back?

She'd expected him to be long gone after she'd made it clear they weren't selling. Who was she kidding? The man didn't give up. He hadn't the first time he'd come to the island and he obviously wasn't now.

She bolstered her resolve. They might be down but they weren't beaten. Nik had called to say both neighbors were horrified by the vandalism and had offered up their water for the Kaapas. Tomorrow men from the Water Department would come and hook up some sort of contraption to bring water to the farm while they went to work repairing the damaged pipe.

So the flowers would be saved.

Now she had to go outside and tell Ryan he'd just better lay off. Not that he'd been all that pushy lately.

In fact, he'd been a rock when she needed one.

This afternoon when he'd slipped his arm around her, she'd almost been reduced to tears, and if they hadn't been surrounded by other people, she might have succumbed.

Having his compassion and support meant the world to her. Though she warned herself not to let it go to her head or her heart, she was having trouble fighting his powerful allure.

Even now, watching him walk toward the house, all long legs clad in lightweight khakis, an aloha shirt left untucked and his dark hair ruffling in the late-afternoon wind, she felt her heart zing and she yearned to throw herself into his arms and ask him to make the world a better place. Her world a safer, more peaceful place. Ridiculous, of course.

But he had made her feel better on numerous occasions of late, which she appreciated and cherished. It wasn't often that she had someone watching her back.

She smoothed her hair away from her face and tightened her ponytail. She had to stay courageous and strong. Reassure him she wasn't going to cave to any pressure and then…he'd leave.

Probably for good.

A dismal ache throbbed in her chest. She wanted to cry, to wallow in the misery of knowing he'd be leaving. Jamming her hands into the pockets of her shorts, she bolstered her flagging self-worth and shook off any sentiment. *Stop it.* Some things couldn't be changed. He had his life. She had hers. End of story.

Forcing herself into action, she opened the front door. Cody came running from the back of the house and pushed past her as she walked onto the porch. The balmy evening wrapped around her, the soothing sound of distant crashing surf and the trill of a night-jar smoothed the edges of her nerves.

Purposely keeping her voice even and unemotional, she said, "Hey, I didn't expect to see you again."

Confusion and hurt flashed in Ryan's eyes as he bent to scratch Cody behind the Aussie's silky ears. "I came back to make sure you and Tutu get safely to a hotel until the water is working again."

Tender affection rose; she tamped it down. "Pano can do that. He should be home from work soon. I paged him."

His eyebrows came together in a slight frown as he stood. "I thought he worked nights?"

She shrugged, not sure how to explain that she really didn't know what was up with Pano. He'd been acting weird lately. But then again, he always acted strangely when intoxicated. "Apparently, he works whenever they need him."

She hoped he didn't work while inebriated. The many horrible accidents that could befall him made her shudder.

Ryan straightened and dragged his hands through his hair, messing the dark strands and making him even more adorable. Her heart gave a kick.

"I just want to help." His dark eyes glowed with an earnestness that made Kiki want to hug him in the worst way. But she refrained. No sense in prolonging the torture.

"And I appreciate your willingness."

An awkward silence stretched between them. Kiki didn't know how to fill in the gap. What could she say or do that would make this any less painful?

"Is Tutu around?" he finally asked, his voice grim.

A burst of anxiousness assaulted her. "Inside. Why? Is something wrong?"

"I'd just like to say goodbye." His voice was soft and full of an emotion she couldn't quite identify.

Kiki swallowed as she fell into the chocolate swirl of his direct gaze. She'd known that this was coming, had thought she was prepared for his departure and yet, the reality of his soon being gone from her life hurt. "When will you leave?"

His gaze moved to the stars visible in the cloudless night sky. "In the morning."

Looking at his profile in the luminescent glow of the moon bathing his features, she tried to learn by heart every line and angle, tucking the memory of his face deep into her heart so she'd always have him close.

He closed his eyes. She wished she could read his mind, for she'd liked to have known what he was thinking, feeling at this precise moment. Was he, too, feeling the bereavement of what could never be?

He turned suddenly, determination etched on his face. "But I want you to know the security company will be out first thing in the morning to install a comprehensive system."

Stunned, her lungs expanded and contracted painfully in her chest. She fought for control of her breathing as his words sank in. "Really, Ryan, we can't afford it right now. Not after all of this." She made a sweeping gesture toward the damaged trucks and the beetle-chewed, dry field.

His voice rough, he replied, "My going-away present to you."

She couldn't have heard him right. Did he just say he'd paid for the security system? He'd hinted at that before, but she hadn't taken him seriously.

Surprise and gratitude and something else that she couldn't identify gripped her, cutting off the oxygen to her brain. She swayed as the world dipped and then righted itself.

Ryan caught her by the elbow. "You okay?"

Thankful for his firm hold, she tried to smile. "Yes. I don't know what happened. I was just dizzy for a sec."

"Here, sit down." He led her to the stairs.

She plopped down on the middle step, liking that he sat close enough to touch. He was solid. Steady. An anchor that she would miss when he left the island. "You have been so good to us. Why?"

One side of his mouth curved upward. "Does there have to be a reason?"

People didn't just do things like this without some ulterior motive. She couldn't imagine what his could be at this point. "Yes. There does."

His dark eyes held her enthralled. "All right. Because I care. Because I don't like to see anyone bullied. Before I leave in the morning I'm going to make sure everyone knows that the offer of purchase for the land has been withdrawn."

He was too good to be real. He seemed to think of everything. "Thank you."

He inclined his head. "The least I can do. That should stop the vandalism."

Forcing herself to turn away from his devastating grin, she stated, "The police still haven't caught the ex-con who's threatened my grandfather." She took his hand and curled her fingers around his. "Thank you for everything."

He squeezed her fingers, his palm flattening against hers, sending warmth up her arm to wrap around her heart. "Will you keep in touch?"

"Sure," the response came automatically, but deep inside she knew that she couldn't. That to do so would only be a torture because… She shied away from analyzing why. "I mean, if you want to keep in touch."

"I would like to very much," he said. "Are you sure I can't escort you and Tutu to a hotel?"

"No. I mean, yes. I mean, you taking us to a hotel would be great." The plain and simple truth was, she wasn't ready to let him walk out of her life. She rose. "We'll need to pack."

He stood. They were on the same stair, just inches from each other. His gaze touched her face and then lowered to her lips as gently as a caress.

A slight shiver of anticipation coursed over her. She leaned closer, waiting, wanting, hoping he'd kiss her. When he closed the distance between them, when his mouth slanted over hers, her heart galloped as sensation after sensation rocketed through her system.

A yearning to melt into his arms overcame her. She slipped her hands over his shoulders and clung to him, deepening the kiss, wishing she never had to let him go, never had to say goodbye.

Slowly, gently, he eased his lips from hers, but his arms still held her close.

Locked within each other's embrace, their gazes melding, Kiki never wanted the moment to end. She wanted to pretend that they could find a future together, but reality stealthily crept into her consciousness when he murmured, "I'll never forget you."

Her life was here, on Maui at the farm. He belonged to a world far away, a world she would never fit into. She knew this and had to accept it as fact.

Disentangling herself from him, she said, "I'll go find Tutu."

She left him standing on the stair, a weighty sadness permanently settled on her shoulders.

* * *

Ryan followed Kiki and her grandmother to one of the smaller hotels that would take dogs along the main drag in Kihei. After depositing their bags in the room and leaving Cody with food and water, he escorted the women to dinner at a local restaurant off the beaten path. Not super high-end, but very comfortable nonetheless.

Kiki suggested he try the Kalua Pork dish or the Ono fish. He elected to try the Ono. Since it was his last night in paradise, he'd step out of his comfort zone and try seafood. He normally wasn't much of a fish lover, much to his Bostonian family's dismay.

He was glad for the extra time with the Kaapa women. He wasn't ready to say goodbye. Every time he thought about getting on the plane in the morning, an ache started to throb deep in his heart.

Something he'd never experienced before and he wasn't too sure he liked the feeling.

And after tomorrow he wouldn't have to feel it again. For some reason that thought didn't offer any comfort.

"Do you like your Ono?" Tutu asked halfway through the meal.

"It's fish," he replied as he looked down at his partially eaten meal. He didn't have much of an appetite. "I really like the cream sauce."

Kiki laughed. "My father's the same way. He'll eat a piece of fish as long as it's smothered in a sauce."

Ryan shared a smile with Kiki. "Sounds like my kind of guy."

"Yes, you and he have some similarities."

Her statement brought him up short. He reached out for her hand, wishing he could say he'd never deny her who she was the way she seemed to feel her father and his family had with her mother. "I hope only good similarities?"

"Yes. All the good ones."

The melancholy expression in Kiki's eyes reflected what he felt. Could she be feeling the same dread at his departure that he was?

He looked down at his plate and pushed his steamed vegetables around with his fork.

Was that why he was not looking forward to going home? Because he...loved Kiki?

His breath froze. His heart knew what it had taken his brain so long to accept. The thought sent his mind careening into a million different directions.

He loved Kiki's courage, her strength, the way her hands moved when she sang the hula or picked a beetle off a hibiscus. He did. He loved her. He was such an idiot for not seeing it sooner.

The arrival of the waiter wanting to take their plates bought Ryan a moment to reflect on the realization that had his heart pounding. He loved Kiki.

Lifting his gaze, he watched her as she and Tutu talked. He tuned out their words and just enjoyed the way Kiki's mouth moved, the way her eyes showed a wonderful display of intelligence and emotion as she chatted.

She glanced at him, her eyes soft and inviting. A look he could get used to if given the chance.

But how could a relationship ever work between them?

His whole life was wrapped up in Boston and hers was on the island. He couldn't ask her to give up her life here when she'd so valiantly fought for it. And he had too much at home to leave. Didn't he? Regret simmered in his soul.

There was no way he could pursue Kiki even to see if her feelings for him ran deep.

Too many miles stood between them.

She said something. He mentally gave himself a shake and focused back on to the conversation. "I'm sorry, can you repeat that?"

"Daydreaming?" she teased, her smile engaging.

"Something like that," he replied, unwilling to confess exactly what he'd been thinking.

"I said it's getting late. We should probably call it an evening."

"Right." He swiped the check the waiter put on the table before Kiki could. He grinned at her. "My treat."

"Thank you." She inclined her head graciously as she scooted her chair out. "I'm going to freshen up."

Ryan nodded, watching the sway of her slim hips beneath her flowing skirt and her long braid that bounced down her back until she disappeared into the women's restroom.

"She's going to miss you."

Tutu's comment brought his attention back to the woman sitting across from him. Tutu looked lovely in her floral dress and with a white jasmine blossom stuck behind one ear.

"I'll miss you both," he hedged, not ready to admit anything more than that. There seemed to be no point.

"I was hoping from the way you two were getting along so well that a romance might be budding."

An inexplicable sense of emptiness settled in his heart. He tried to keep his face from revealing the bleakness he felt deep inside.

She sighed. "But I guess not. You must be looking forward to getting back to your family."

"Yes. It will be good to see my mom and siblings." Only he'd be leaving a part of himself behind.

Kiki came rushing back, her cell phone in her hand, and her eyes wide and anxious. Ryan and Tutu stood. "What's wrong?"

"My father called. The man stalking my grandfather tried to kill him and my grandmother last night." She swallowed. Tutu slipped her arm around Kiki. "The FBI caught the guy and Grandmother is fine, but Grandfather has suffered a stroke. The doctors said they won't know how much damage has been done for a few days."

Aching for her, Ryan took her hand. "Do you need to go there?"

"Daddy said no. That there wasn't any point to going right now," she said. "Grandfather and I were never close, but I still feel horrible that this has happened to him."

"Of course you do, dear," Tutu murmured. "It's just awful."

At least *that* threat was now gone. And tomorrow after he contacted all the neighbors, the Kaapa women would be left in peace. Ryan could leave knowing that Kiki was truly safe.

He walked the ladies back to their hotel. In the austere lobby, that was thankfully empty, he stopped. "I'll say goodbye here," he stated, knowing that it would be better to just make the break as quickly and as cleanly as possible.

Tutu gave him a hug. The scent of jasmine wafted from the flower at her ear, imprinting this moment in his mind.

"Be safe," she said as she released him. "Kiki, I'll wait for you upstairs."

Tutu disappeared up the staircase leading to the second floor, where their room was located.

Kiki's smile wavered a bit. "If you ever come back, you'll have to come visit us."

"Without question," he replied, wishing he didn't feel so torn up inside.

Falling in love hadn't been in his plan when he

came to Maui. In fact, finding a wife wasn't in the plan for at least a few more years, not until he'd reached his financial goals.

He knew his brothers would say that God was the one in control. That His plans were far better than anything we could dream up. But why would God allow him to fall in love with Kiki if there was no way for them to have a future together?

"Well, I guess I should say goodbye," he said, hating how much he hurt inside.

She nodded and touched his face, her palm warm against his cheek. "I'll never forget you."

She turned and fled up the stairs and out of sight.

With a heavy heart, Ryan left the hotel to go back to his rented condo.

Kiki couldn't relax even though she sat curled on the bed, the blue floral spread pulled over her feet, with Tutu sitting beside her watching the news. Kiki's mind was too keyed up with all that had happened in the last few days.

The farm had been at turns sabotaged and vandalized, her car was still in the auto shop being repaired and Ryan was leaving in the morning.

The fact that she didn't want him to leave made her hurt deep in her heart in a way that she'd never ached before. Not even when she broke off her relationship with her ex-boyfriend. She'd been hurt, but now she realized it had been her pride more than her heart.

Now she understood a broken heart.

Only Ryan hadn't really broken her heart. Kiki had done that all on her own.

She'd gone and fallen in love with him. And hadn't even told him, hadn't given him a chance to accept or reject her. She didn't want to analyze what that said about her. Maybe deep inside she feared rejection. Or feared that he, too, felt the connection, the love that she felt. But what good would knowing either way do? A future together wasn't possible.

What was done was done. She'd lived with heartache in one form or another all her life until she found her place on the Kaapa Flower Farm.

She got up off the bed. Maybe some work would help. She could look over the upcoming orders and see whose orders she could delay for a few days until everything at the farm was up and running. Ugh! She'd forgotten her laptop.

"I'm going to run back to the house for my laptop," she said, slipping on her sandals. Since she hadn't changed from her skirt and tank from earlier, she could just grab the keys to her grandmother's car and go.

Tutu switched off the television. "I'll come with you."

Cody rose from the foot of the bed and moved to the door.

"You, too, boy?" Kiki chuckled, grateful she'd thought of a dog for protection and companionship.

She really loved Cody. Loved the way he seemed to understand her when she talked and understand when to give her space. Not as good as a human relationship but at least a relationship. "Okay. Let's go."

The three of them all piled into the Mercedes sedan. Kiki drove them back to the farm. Once there, they all got out. Cody ran off toward the back while Kiki and Tutu headed inside.

Tutu went straight to the answering machine on the sideboard in the living room and hit the playback button. Pano's voice filled the living room.

"Hey. Got your message. I'll go to my own place. Glad to hear you two are staying at a hotel. Talk to you tomorrow."

Kiki snorted as she unplugged her laptop from the printer and slid it into a carrying case. "Good thing we didn't rely on him tonight."

"Kiki," Tutu said reprovingly.

She shrugged. "Sorry. He's just been so weird and unavailable. Not that he isn't normally, but you'd think with all that we've been going through he'd—"

An explosion rocked the house, the violent force slamming Kiki to her knees.

This was it, she thought. This really was the end. They were going to lose everything. Including their lives.

TWELVE

Panic zapped Kiki's nerve endings and flooded her system with adrenaline. The noise of the blast rang in her ears. The windows shattered. Doors, cabinetry and hunks of the walls and ceiling went flying. Tutu screamed and dropped to the ground, her hands over her head.

Black smoke billowed in through the broken windows. Outside, Cody pawed at the front door, barking wildly to get in.

But they had to get *out* of the house!

Kiki grabbed Tutu by the arm and led her to the door. The minute she flung the door open, Cody rushed in, his barks frantic.

"No!" Kiki rushed Tutu outside and down the porch where the smoke and heat from the house wasn't nearly as overwhelming. Then Kiki ran back inside for Cody.

He stood barking at the fire now engulfing the back of the house. Kiki grabbed him by the collar and dragged him toward safety. Acrid smoke filled her lungs, burning her insides. She clamped a hand over her mouth, trying to fliter the air with her fingers.

Just as she and Cody crossed the threshold of the door a chunk of the ceiling fell, catching Kiki's heel and tripping her. She flew forward. Releasing her grasp on Cody, she tried to break her fall with her hands. She hit the porch hard. Pain shot up her left arm. She forced herself to crawl off the porch and down the stairs.

"Kiki!" Tutu rushed to her side, tears streaming down her face.

With Tutu's help, Kiki managed to sit, cradling her arm. "I'm okay. But I think my arm's broken."

Tutu released her hold on Kiki and sank to the ground clutching a hand over heart. "I...don't think...I am."

Fresh panic and fear slammed into Kiki with the force of a sledgehammer.

She scrambled closer, putting her unhurt arm around Tutu. Cody sat close, too, as if instinctively knowing they needed all the support they could get. "Oh, God, please help us," Kiki whispered.

Knowing she couldn't just sit there and let her grandmother suffer, Kiki said, "My cell's in the car. I'm going to call for help."

She forced herself to her feet. For a moment the world spun crazily before focusing once again. She staggered to the car and managed to get the phone. Within seconds she had the 9-1-1 operator on the line.

"Hurry, please. There's been an explosion at my house. There is a fire, and my grandmother…" A sob broke through. "I think she's having a heart attack."

The operator promised the EMTs were on their way, along with the fire department and the police.

Kiki rushed back to her grandmother. Tutu had fallen sideways to the ground. Cody licked her face as if trying to wake her. Choking on her tears, Kiki knelt beside Tutu and checked her pulse. Thready but there.

Kiki prayed for a miracle.

And really, really wished Ryan were with them. She could use his steady strength.

But he wasn't. He'd left. She was going to have to rely on her own strength.

Sleep had proved impossible, so now Ryan sat slumped in a chair on the lanai of his rented condo, staring out at the dark ocean, listening to the crashing surf as the waves tumbled against the shoreline of Keawakapu. From the cluster of trees off to the left, nocturnal birds trilled a serenade, as sad and lonely a tune as Ryan had ever heard. His heart ached in rhythm with the sounds of the night.

In five hours he was to board a plane and fly back to Boston. Back to his world.

He would miss this island paradise, but more than that, he would miss his island girl. But her life was here.

His office, his family, his life were in Boston.

He thought about his brother Patrick and how Patrick had sacrificed everything to be with Anne. He'd walked away from his career, his friends and his family because Anne had been in the witness protection program and a madman had vowed to kill her for testifying against him in a murder trial. For five months there had been no contact with Patrick. He hadn't even been able to tell his family that he'd married Anne.

At the time, Ryan hadn't understood how Patrick could surrender everything for love. But now...

Ryan sat up straighter. Would it really be a sacrifice to move his office to Maui? He wouldn't have to give up all contact with his family the way Patrick had done. He could hop on a plane anytime and fly back, or they could visit there.

But the questions that tore through him and halted his suddenly optimistic plans were, would Kiki want him to stay? Would she want him in her life?

The sound of his cell phone ringing interrupted his worried thoughts. He checked the caller ID and didn't recognize the number.

"Hello?"

"McClain, Abiko here. There's been an explosion and fire at the Kaapa house. Kiki and Auntie Lana are at the hospital."

Ryan's knees buckled and he sank into the chair. His heart squeezed tight. *Please, Father in heaven, don't let them be...* He couldn't bring himself to even think the word that tried to cut through his mind. "Is she... Are they..."

"Kiki's got a broken arm but is otherwise okay. Auntie Lana had a heart attack," Nik replied, his voice sounding strained. "Let me give you directions to the hospital."

Relieved they weren't dead, as he'd feared, Ryan listened, absorbing the information. What were they doing back at the house?

"Thanks for calling. I'm on my way," Ryan said as he slipped on his shoes and swiped his keys from the table before heading out the door.

"Yeah, well, I figured you'd want to know, seeing how close you two have become."

Had his feelings been that obvious? "You're right. I'm on my way." He flipped the phone closed as he ran for his car.

Ryan left his rented car in front of the five-story, V-shaped Maui Medical Center's emergency doors in the middle of the circular driveway.

A uniformed guard rushed at him. "You can't park your car there."

Ryan tossed the man his keys. "Don't have time."

He had to see if Kiki and Tutu were okay. Ever since Nik called him a half hour ago and explained that an explosion had sent the Kaapa women to the hospital, Ryan had berated himself for not making sure the ladies hadn't left anything behind they might need. Nik said they'd gone back to get Kiki's laptop. He should have thought of that.

Ryan skidded to a halt at the administration desk. "Kaapa?"

The young blonde behind the desk smiled as her fingers clicked over the keys on her desktop computer. "Floor four, east wing, room 404."

"Thanks," Ryan said, and bolted for the elevator.

On the fourth floor, he practically ran down the hall, looking for the correct room number. There on his left.

He slowed and took several deep breaths to calm his racing heart. As he entered the room, his gaze snagged on Kiki sitting on a chair beside her grandmother's bed.

Kiki's left arm was in a cast, her eyes red and swollen from crying, but she was still as beautiful as ever. Tutu lay sleeping, her face ashen beneath her brown skin.

He forced himself not to rush forward and pull her to him. Her eyes widened when she saw him. She jumped to her feet and practically flung herself into his arms.

He held her close, the lingering scent of smoke making tears clog his throat. He could have lost her this night. He wasn't going to lose her again.

"You're okay?" he managed to ask around the lump in his throat.

She nodded. "But Tutu had a mild heart attack."

He looked over Kiki's head toward the bed. "Will she be all right?"

"Yes. The doctors are confident that she hasn't suffered any permanent damage."

"Have you called your parents?"

"Yes. Mom's going to fly out today. Dad has to stay with Grandfather."

"What happened to your arm?"

She waved the casted limb slightly. "Broken. The doctor said it was a clean break and should heal nicely."

She could have been hurt so much worse. Just the thought of how much worse made him break out in a cold sweat. "And Cody?"

"He's fine. One of the EMTs said he'd take care of him for me." She pulled away from Ryan and moved to the window. "This is such a mess. Why does life have to be so hard?"

Ryan moved to stand behind her, his hands coming to rest on her shoulders. He needed the physical contact to assure himself she was truly okay. "Remember what Pastor Gerome said about trusting God in His abiding presence? I think now is a good time to put that into practice. I don't know why all this stuff is happening, but I think God would want you, us, to put our faith and our trust in Him."

"'Be strong and of good courage,'" she whispered.

"Exactly," he said, smoothing back her hair with

one hand. She sagged back against him. "I'm so glad you're here."

"I came as soon as Nik called."

"That was good of him." She turned in his arms. "But what about your flight reservations?"

All plans to leave were forgotten the second Nik called and told him about the explosion, but he wasn't ready to tell her he wasn't going anywhere. This didn't seem the time or place for that discussion. He shrugged. "Don't worry about it."

A noise from the doorway drew their attention. Nik stood on the threshold, his expression grim, his dark eyes hard. Ryan stepped back to allow Kiki room as she moved away from the window and walked toward her friend. The officer gave her a quick hug and then motioned for her and Ryan to follow him out into the hall.

"The forensic team found a bomb, similar to the pipe bomb planted in the fertilizer truck. It apparently was attached to the back wall of the house, connected to a timer."

Rage seethed in Ryan all the way to his bones. Someone had deliberately burned down the Kaapa house. Only one person with motive came to Ryan's mind. Horatio.

Not wanting to upset Kiki, Ryan kept his thoughts to himself. As soon as he could snag a moment alone with Nik, Ryan had an idea on how to trap Horatio.

"I'm sorry to say your house is completely gone," Nik said, his voice echoing his sympathy.

Sadness filled Kiki's eyes and tears slipped down her cheeks. "There were a lot of memories in that house."

"Yes, there were," Nik agreed. He looked past them and tipped his chin.

Ryan turned to see Pano barreling down the hall, his broad face a mask of terror. He stumbled to a halt beside Kiki, his gaze searching her. "You okay?"

"Yes." She wrinkled her nose. "Oh, Pano. You've been drinking again."

Ryan and Nik exchanged concerned glances. Ryan wasn't sure what type of drunk Pano was—a mean one or a sloppy one. Either way, the last thing Kiki needed was having to deal with her inebriated cousin.

"I want to see Tutu," Pano said, his voice shaky.

Ryan took his arm. "Not right now, not like this."

Pano shook him off. "Lay off, Haole boy. I don't need your permission."

Nik stepped closer. "Pano, let's go sober you up."

Pano pushed Nik back. "I don't need you telling me what to do, either." Pano turned his wild-eyed gaze back on Kiki. "Is she okay?"

"She will be. She had a mild heart attack," Kiki answered.

Pano shook his head. "What were you two doing there? You were supposed to be at a hotel."

"We went back for my laptop," Kiki said as fresh tears gathered in her eyes.

Ryan put his hand to the small of her back to offer her support. She leaned closer. He hated that she was hurting and obviously blaming herself, especially since he was pretty sure who was to blame.

Nik took Pano by the arm. "Let's get you some coffee. Excuse us, Kiki, Ryan."

Pano jerked his arm out of Nik's gasp. "I don't need coffee. I'm going to see Tutu." He stormed into the room, leaving them all staring after him.

"He'll sober up soon enough," Nik said. "He's not as bad as I've seen him."

"He needs help," Kiki stated, her gaze on the empty doorway.

"He does. But right now you have to think about what you and Tutu are going to do," Nik said.

Ryan planned on being in on that discussion but now was not the time to say so. "Thanks for calling me earlier," he said to Nik.

A slight smile played at his mouth. "Figured you'd want to know." Nik turned to Kiki. "I'll let you know if I find out anything else. If you'll both excuse me…" Nik sauntered away.

Seeing this as a prime time to offer his plan to Nik, Ryan gave Kiki a squeeze before releasing her. "I've got to go, too."

He took off after Nik. If all went as he hoped, by the time he came back, Horatio would be in jail.

And then Kiki and Ryan would be free to find out what the future held for them.

Kiki blinked back fresh tears at Ryan's sudden departure. *I've got to go, too.* What kind of goodbye was that?

She watched as he and Nik disappeared into the elevator. So much for his support.

"You got it bad for him," Pano stated, his words slightly slurred.

She jerked her gaze to where he stood, slouched against the door frame of their grandmother's hospital room. His words hit the mark and she backpedaled. "No. Of course not."

Pano snorted. "Liar."

She glared at him. "I'm not a liar. So maybe I do like him. So what?"

"Right. So what? As long as Kiki gets what she wants," Pano sneered, and pushed away from the frame. "You're to blame for Tutu's heart attack. If you'd just sold the farm in the first place, none of this would have happened."

Kiki gritted her teeth. She wasn't going to argue with him while he was drunk and unreasonable. She moved to go back in to Tutu's room but he blocked her path.

"Miss High and Mighty, with her rich daddy's money, coming to the Kaapa Flower Farm to rescue us poor slobs," Pano jeered.

Kiki stepped back, not liking his words or the menacing way they were said. "Pano, you don't know what you're talking about."

"I know that if you hadn't come back, Tutu would have sold the farm. She's old and tired of running that dead horse. But noooo, along comes Miss Know It All to save the day. Well, no one wanted you to save anything. The developer is willing to pay top dollar for the land. And we need that money."

What did Pano mean? Did he think he was entitled to some of the profits of the sale? She bristled. "You know even if Tutu had sold the farm, you wouldn't have received a dime."

His dark eyes flashed with hatred. Kiki staggered back another step. Whoa. Was that just the alcohol or did he really harbor ill feelings toward her?

She held up a hand. "Let's get something straight, cousin," she said, her voice hard. "Tutu has made me trustee of her living trust, which means I have control of the estate. And as long as she is alive, her money is hers."

A cagey expression crossed his features. "What happens if you die?"

She couldn't help staring at him slack-jawed. "What?"

"You heard me. What happens if you die?"

Not liking the gurgle of fear churning in her stomach, she said, "There would be a new trustee."

She decided to refrain from telling him that her

mother was the successor trustee named in the living trust. In order to draw him out, she asked, "Do you need money?"

His lip curled. "Yeah. We all need money, but we all don't have a wealthy father bankrolling our life."

"Is that what you think? That my father bankrolled my life?"

"How else would you have gotten to go to that fancy college or start that Web business or travel back and forth between here and there so often, huh?"

She straightened her spine. "First, I earned a scholarship to that 'fancy' college and second, I earned the money to go into business. With a partner. And third, yeah, my father flew me back and forth growing up. I can't change the choices they made. And I can't change that your parents died."

Hurt crept into the edges of his eyes. "Yeah, well. Neither can I." He ran a hand through his hair, leaving grooves where his thick fingers dug in.

Empathy for the boy she'd been raised with blunted the sharpness of his attack against her. "Why do you need money?"

"I owe some people money. Some not very nice people." His shoulders slumped.

A knot tightened in her chest. "Money for what?"

"My Jeep and stuff. These people want their money back. I don't have it." Desperation etched lines in his face.

"But you make good money working for the state." He seemed to be working so much; how could he not have money enough to pay off his debt?

His expression fell, making him look so much like he had as a young boy. "I was fired a month ago for drinking on the job."

"Kiki?"

Tutu's weak voice drifted into the hall. The two cousins hurried back into the hospital room. The bleak, white walls and the beeping of the heart monitor made Kiki shiver. She hated that Tutu was lying in that bed.

Pano was right, it was Kiki's fault. Guilt stung her like the dreaded end of a wasp. If she had thought beyond her own desire to save her heritage, Tutu could be living a very comfortable life right now, not stretched out on a bed, hooked up to a machine. Remorse spread over her, hot and burning like lava down the side of a mountain.

Self-blame and sorrow clawed at Kiki as she took Tutu's fragile hand in hers. "I'm so sorry, Tutu," she whispered.

Tutu smiled softly. "Not your fault." Her gaze shifted to Pano. "Glad you're here. And safe."

Pano bent over to kiss Tutu's cheek; the foul odors from too much partying made Kiki's head spin.

Tutu's gaze narrowed. "You've been drinking."

Kiki bit her lip, wishing Pano hadn't arrived reeking of booze. That he'd at least thought about his condition before rushing to the hospital.

"Sorry," he mumbled.

"How many times have I told you that alcohol will only get you into trouble," she said. A sheen of sweat broke out on her forehead.

"Tutu, please, don't excite yourself," Kiki said, concern jolting through her.

"It just saddens me," she whispered as an alarm on the monitor gave a loud shrill. Tutu's eyes closed, her hand went limp within Kiki's grasp.

"Tutu!"

People rushed into the room. A nurse hustled Kiki and Pano out in to the hall. Pano lumbered toward the elevator, his gait unsteady as he wiped at his tears.

Tears streamed down Kiki's face, as well. Terror that she'd lose Tutu made her heart clench and her breathing was labored.

She longed for Ryan to return, to be the rock she needed, but he'd left. And she was alone.

To make a decision that would change her future.

THIRTEEN

Ryan sat near Nik's desk in the Maui Police Department building, staring out the window that overlooked the front entrance. Two stunning trees graced the front lawn, their red, orange and yellow hand-size, tulip-shaped blossoms bobbing gently in the midday sun.

Ryan wondered if Kiki had ever thought of planting trees like these on the Kaapa property. He liked how the trunk was thick and bare until the branches spread out in a vertical fashion with the green leaves and colorful flowers making a canopy effect under the tree.

"Here we go," Nik said as he sauntered back to his desk. "The Chief and the D.A. gave the go-ahead. You make the call." He slid the black desk phone over toward Ryan.

"Do you have the number of the Fairmont?" Ryan asked, adrenaline building in his chest.

They were really going to do it. They were going

to pull off a sting operation. Ryan was to call Horatio and ask for one last meeting. Then Ryan, wearing a wire, would get Horatio to admit to the sabotage and vandalism.

Not that Ryan thought Horatio had committed the crime himself; he surely hired someone else. But if they could get him to admit to that, he'd be arrested for conspiracy at the least. Then all this nasty business would end.

And his future with Kiki would hopefully begin.

Nik pulled out the phone book and flipped through until he came to the page with the Fairmont Kea Lani Hotel's ad. Ryan dialed the number and asked for Horatio's room.

Horatio answered on the second ring. "Yes."

"Horatio, it's Ryan."

"You have good news?"

Ryan's lip curled. "Maybe. I need face time. I'll come to your hotel in an hour."

"Fine. I'll be here."

Ryan hung up.

"Good job. Nice and cool," Nik said as he rose. "Let's get you to tactical. They will set you up with a wire and a vest."

Ryan frowned as unease slithered over him. "I don't think he'd shoot me."

"I've learned it's best to be prepared," Nik answered, and led the way through the station.

Ryan really wished his brother Brody, the sheriff,

were here walking him through this. Not that Ryan didn't trust Nik, but if anything were to go wrong, Ryan would sure rather count on his brother to have his back.

"Okay, God, I'm going to trust that You have my back," he murmured. *Be strong and of good courage.*

Kiki hesitated outside the hotel suite's double doors. The sun glinted off the brass knocker and reflected in the pristine white stuccoed walls of the multitiered, all-suite Fairmont Kea Lani Hotel resort. Taking deep bracing breaths, she tried to steady her nerves and her hands before committing herself. Once she knocked, there'd be no going back. Once she entered the suite her fate was sealed.

But for her grandmother's sake, Kiki was going to do what needed to be done. She was going to accept Mr. Lewis's offer for the Kaapa land.

She would have much preferred to have worked through Ryan but, she hadn't been able to reach him after he left the hospital. She assumed he was on a plane right now, flying over the Pacific Ocean.

Maybe one day she'd fly over to Boston to see him. Or not. Since he left without a proper goodbye, she could only assume that meant a visit wouldn't be welcome. Her heart twisted in her chest with sad regret.

Okay, come on. Stop the melancholy and get on with it. She lifted her hand and used the oval ring to knock.

A moment later the door opened. Horatio Lewis, looking much as she had last seen him, greeted her with a smile. "I'm so glad you called. Please, come in."

Trying to fight the urge to bolt, Kiki stepped into the plush, lavishly decorated suite. Soothing beige walls, with lightweight silk drapes outlining the magnificent wall of windows that gave a panoramic view of the blue-green Pacific Ocean, captivated her.

White slip-covered sofas with ecru-colored accent pillows faced a gas fireplace. Bamboo floors with Persian throw rugs made Kiki feel as if she were gliding rather than walking. She'd never before seen such opulence. Not even in Philadelphia.

There was money there, yes, old money with old furnishings worth more than she could guess, but this…this was luxury in a way she'd never experienced. A bath to the left, with creamy marble fixtures and ambient lighting made her pause.

She caught a glimpse of the bedroom through the bamboo louvered doors. A huge four-poster bed on a platform rose in the center of the room. Crisp white linens with a soft pale green blanket folded neatly across the bed made Kiki wonder if the bed was as comfy as it looked with its fluffy pillows.

With the sale of the property, her Tutu could live like this. Could have all these luxuries that she could never have had on the farm.

Kiki stiffened her resolve. She forced her attention to the man now leading her to the lanai through a set of double sliding doors. Wooden containers of blooming begonias waved prettily at her as she sat at the white metal table.

"Would you care for tea?" Horatio asked, indicating a large glass pitcher of iced tea.

Rings of oranges floated at the top, making Kiki's mouth water. Her stomach rumbled, reminding her that she hadn't eaten thus far today. She nodded and waited as he poured her a tall glass of the delicious, amber-colored liquid. Taking a sip, she let the refreshing burst of flavor slide down her throat and settle her stomach.

After a moment, she set the drink aside. Best to get on with this. "I've decided to accept your offer."

Horatio sat back with a pleased smile on his weathered face. "Now that is a bit of good news. Ryan said he had some and I was quite surprised when you called, since I figured you would want to deal through him. But no matter, he'll still get his bonus when he arrives."

Stunned, she stared, trying to make sense of what he'd just said. "Ryan called you? When? Arrives? As in here?"

"Yes. Earlier. Yes. And anytime now," Horatio answered, a twinkle glinting in his eyes behind his thick glasses.

Ryan was coming here? He'd said he had good news? He'd known she'd cave?

She'd been played. Thoroughly had, like some simpleton. Anger heated her skin until she thought she'd burst into flames right on the spot. Another, more sinister thought crept into her mind with taunting clarity. Had Ryan orchestrated all the sabotage and vandalism, the destruction of her home in order to secure the deal?

She'd really thought he cared. She'd thought she knew him. But obviously the generous honorable man that he'd presented to her had been a facade. A well-acted, well-executed facade.

Her hands balled into tight fists. "I'd just as soon not see Ryan. Do you have the documents for me to sign?"

He stood. "I do." He disappeared inside the suite.

Kiki stared out at the ocean but the view was blurry through the tears gathering in her eyes. Vaguely she heard a knock and then the sound of voices. She cringed then straightened. She may have been fooled once but not again. Rising from her chair, she turned to see Ryan walking toward her, a strange, horrified expression on his face.

He stopped in front of her and gathered her hands in his. "What are you doing here, Kiki?"

"I could ask you the same question, but frankly I don't care. I just want this over with now." She yanked her hands from his. She pressed them together to keep them from shaking.

"No. You are not signing those papers," Ryan said, his jaw hard and his dark eyes intense.

She frowned, confused. "I thought that was what you wanted? For your bonus?"

"And I told you, not like this."

He turned to face Horatio and blocked her view of the older man. What was he doing? The gesture seemed protective but so odd. She pushed past him. "Where do I sign?"

"Don't you need Tutu's signature?" Ryan asked, his voice carrying a note of desperation.

Trying to wrap her mind around the situation, she shook her head. "I'm the trustee for her living will. She is incapacitated and may be for a while. She suffered another attack after you left the hospital."

Sympathy and anger warred in Ryan's gaze. "This is not a good time to make a rash decision, Kiki."

"It's not rash." She began signing while keeping half her attention on Ryan. What was up with him?

Ryan's expression seemed to still into resignation before he turned his full attention to Horatio. "You did it. You forced her hand."

The older man frowned. "I don't know what you mean."

"Sure you do. Oh, I know you didn't do the dirty work yourself. But how much does one pay to build a pipe bomb and blow up a truck? Or slash tires? Or burn down a house?"

Kiki stopped signing. A chill ran down her arms chasing away the warmth of the high sun.

Horatio held up his hands. "Hey, I admit that all those helped the cause but I didn't think them up."

"But you paid for them to happen," Ryan pressed.

Kiki watched Horatio closely. His eyes shifted ever so much before he spoke.

"Now, I haven't paid anyone anything."

He was lying. Deep inside, Kiki knew the man was behind it all. Not Ryan. Relief swept through her. She should have never doubted Ryan. Shame for doing so ate away at her relief. She grabbed the papers and began to rip them up.

"No, no!" Horatio said, trying to stop her.

Ryan grabbed Horatio by the arm and forced him back. "Kiki, you need to leave now."

She frowned, not wanting to leave him. "You come with me."

"I'll see you back at the hospital. My business isn't finished here."

The intense way he looked at her as if to say *go with me on this* had her nodding and backing out. With the torn papers in hand, she fled the suite. Once outside, she briskly made her way through the hotel and to the concierge.

"Do you have a shredding machine?" she asked the brunette woman behind the desk. The name tag on her A-line, knee-length, floral dress said Haley.

Haley smiled. "Yes. Would you like to come to the business center? Sometimes our guests prefer to do their own shredding, or I can take it for you if you would prefer."

"I'll do it myself," Kiki said, and followed Haley to the business center. Faxes whirred and printers hummed. Haley showed Kiki the machine and then left her to do her shredding.

Once she'd made confetti of the contract, Kiki walked outside to the parking lot and to her grandmother's car. She looked around for Ryan's rental, but decided a white Mustang must be the flavor of the year. There were so many in all colors, with white being a more popular one.

Maybe she'd just wait until he came out.

Her cell phone trilled. She unhooked it from her waist and looked at the incoming number. Pano.

She answered. "Are you back at the hospital? Is Tutu okay?"

"I'm not at the hospital, I'm at the farm. The greenhouse suffered some damage during the fire and I think you better come decide what to do with your plants."

She hit the roof of her grandmother's Mercedes with her open palm. "Ugh. I'll be right there."

She clicked off and got in the car.

So much for waiting for Ryan. She'd have to see him later. And later, she would tell him just how she felt about him.

Ryan was sweating.

He could feel droplets running down his back beneath the Kevlar vest. He sure hoped that the wire wouldn't short out and goose him. Once the door to the suite closed behind Kiki, Ryan assumed a casual pose under the shade of the tall palm growing just off to the left of the lanai.

Since Nik and the other officers hadn't come piling in yet, Ryan guessed they didn't have enough "evidence" on tape to make an arrest.

Folding his arms akimbo, Ryan said, "So you said you haven't paid anyone anything. But you're planning to. How much? I may want to use the same technique some day and would like to know what to expect."

Horatio scoffed. "You don't fool me, boy. That Boy Scout honor code you live by wouldn't allow you to do whatever was necessary to get the job done."

He hadn't learned to be honorable from the Boy Scouts, but from his father via his two older brothers. But a man as unscrupulous as Horatio wouldn't understand, so Ryan didn't even try to explain. Instead, he said, "Did you bring a guy over from the mainland? Or did you hire a local?"

Horatio snorted. "As local as they get."

Ryan stilled. That sounded like a confession to him, but no doors were busting open. "A neighbor? Which one?"

Horatio poured himself a glass of iced tea. "No neighbors. The Kaapa fellow. You know the drunk one."

If the railing weren't holding Ryan up, he'd have fallen over. "You hired Pano?"

"He called me last month, drunker than a skunk, going on about how his granny would sell if it weren't for his meddling cousin. Said he'd make sure they had to sell, for a price. I told him you were heading over with the paperwork and once the deal was signed, if he had a hand in the negotiations, I'd give him 5k."

Ryan couldn't believe his ears. For a lousy five thousand dollars, Pano had blown up his grandmother's home, not to mention all the other things he'd damaged. Processing through what Horatio said, Ryan asked, "So he knew I was coming?"

"Right down to when your plane arrived."

So Ryan being at the farm when the fertilizer truck exploded hadn't been coincidence but part of Pano's plan to convince Kiki to sign the documents. Smoldering rage made his insides burn. Ryan pushed away from the railing. "Did Pano tell you what he planned to do to earn that 5K?"

Horatio shook his head. "I didn't want to know. Doesn't matter now because this deal has definitely gone south."

"Yes, it has. But Pano doesn't know that," Ryan said, and walked out of the suite on wobbly legs.

In the hall Nik was waiting with his men. At Nik's motion, two officers entered the suite to arrest Horatio. Ryan didn't plan on hanging around to see how Horatio reacted. Ryan's only concern was Kiki.

One look in Nik's eyes told Ryan the man was

feeling the same amount of shock at Pano's deceit and the same amount of dread for Kiki's safety.

"We have to find Kiki," Ryan stated, his voice urgent. Thoughts of what could happen filled his brain and made his heart pitch.

"I've already called the hospital, she hasn't shown back up there yet. They'll call if she does," Nik said.

Ryan, with Nik at his heels, raced down the stairs to the lobby. Guests and employees scattered as they blew out the doors into the hot sun.

Ryan could only think of one other place she'd go. The farm.

He sent up a prayer that they'd find her before anything bad happened to her.

Kiki stared, transfixed at the carnage left by the fire. Smoke still rose from the charred, gutted remains of the house. The lingering acrid stench of smoke was strong enough to overpower the farm's earthy scents.

A house they could rebuild. But Tutu's life hung in the balance. It wasn't fair. Kiki didn't know what could be done to Horatio Lewis but she'd make sure he paid for this. For hurting her grandmother.

She left a message at the police station for Nik. Hopefully they could arrest Horatio for something.

But she didn't want to take the time now to file a formal complaint; all she'd wanted was to save what she could of her prized orchids.

Her gaze shifted to the greenhouse. She frowned. It looked intact. She went for a closer inspection. There were no burn marks, no charred beams or even broken glass. The padlock she'd bought was still locked.

Why had Pano said that the greenhouse had been damaged? And where was he? His Jeep wasn't in the driveway as she'd expected. Maybe he'd been drinking again and hallucinated.

In which case she hoped he wasn't driving. She shuddered. When this was all settled, she'd try to talk him into going to a treatment center or AA or something.

"Kiki!"

She spun around so fast pain shot through her broken arm to her shoulder and made her wince. Her gaze searched for her cousin. She was sure she'd just heard his voice. But he was nowhere to be seen. The fields were empty. Maybe the shed or the barn.

She walked toward the big metal building they called the barn, but really was the work area for the employees who prepared the leis, the floral arrangements and the cut stemmed flowers for transport.

The building was dark. "Pano?"

No answer.

She moved to the small wooden shed at the back of the property, where her grandfather had kept all of his personal wood carving tools. She remembered as a child loving to watch as he'd carve into a piece

of hala or banyan tree to make intricately detailed de-
signs that he'd toss away or give to the kids. He whit-
tled for relaxation, not money, he'd say.

Kiki used to have several pieces sitting on her
nightstand. But now they were just ash. Grief and
anger pounded through her blood. So much lost.

The shed was empty, as well. Just as she was turning to leave, something shoved her hard from behind,
sending her sprawling across the dusty wooden floor.
She cried out as her broken arm smacked against the
hard surface and her forehead connected with the
edge of a wooden chest.

White dots spun through her vision as she tried to
right herself. Part of her brain knew she needed to determine the threat to protect herself, but the rest of
her brain was trying to deal with the pain ricochet-
ing through her body.

Two dirt-covered, sandal-clad feet appeared in her
line of vision. Blinking, she gazed up and into the
dark and feral eyes of her cousin.

FOURTEEN

"Pano? What…why?" Outrage and confusion made her blood pound harder, increasing the pain in her arm.

He grabbed her by the braid and yanked her head back. He leaned in close, his breath reeking of fresh alcohol. "You're standing in my way."

"The way of what? I don't understand," she said, trying to make sense of his actions. Why would Pano deliberately hurt her? She'd known he was jealous of her, but she hadn't realized that his jealousy would turn so malicious.

He released her with a shove. Her head snapped forward, sending fresh waves of agony coursing through her system. Disbelief that this was happening tried to steal her thoughts. How could her cousin be so mean?

Come on, concentrate. Widening her eyes to help bring Pano into focus, she assessed the situation through a brain cloudy with incredulity. And it didn't look good.

Pano stood between her and the door. The only exit.

His bulky frame hunched and menacing. She barely recognized the man in his eyes. He regarded her with murder in their dark depths. Terror clawed at her. With only one good arm, how could she fight her way out?

She scooted farther from Pano and closer to the workbench. "What is it you hope to gain by hurting me?"

"I checked into this 'living will' thing. If the trustee is gone, then Tutu will have to appoint another trustee. Who do you think she'll appoint?"

Kiki stomach pitched. He thought if he killed her, he'd gain access to Tutu's money? He was so wrong. Her mother was next in line. And he might try to get rid of her, too. Kiki would never put her mother in jeopardy. "You can't just kill me. You'll never be the trustee from prison."

"Oh, I don't plan on going to prison." He moved to pick up a can from near the door, opened the spout and then began liberally sprinkling solvent over the floor and on the walls near the door.

The strong odor made Kiki gag and she watched in horror as he took out a set of matches. Paralyzing fear rammed into her solar plexus.

"Pano, no. Please don't do this. Can't we talk this through? I'm sure we can come to some agreement," she said, hoping to buy some time. She levered herself up with her good arm and managed to hoist herself to her feet to lean against the workbench.

"You made it clear earlier, Kiki, that I won't see a dime as long as you're alive." He grinned sadistically. "By your own mouth you told me what I had to do."

Drunk and mentally unstable. Great. She frantically searched for some way to stop him. Her gaze landed on the pitchfork leaning against the wall beside the workbench. "I was being unreasonable then. You have to understand, I was upset. Afraid that Tutu would die." She inched over so she was in front of the pitchfork.

"I wasn't thinking clearly," she said. "But I am now. Tell me what you need, Pano. I'll make sure you get it," she said as her good hand curled around the long handle of the tool.

"Why should I believe you," he said, his eyes narrowing.

Slowly she took a step forward, dragging the pitchfork behind her. Only the barest sound of the metal prongs scraping along the floor rose. "Because `ohana. We're family. We have to help each other. I want to help."

With each word she inched forward, dragging the pitchfork with her, careful to keep the handle close to her back so he wouldn't see it. "I wish you'd come to me sooner. If I'd known that you were having problems, I would have helped."

"I'm not having problems," he growled, and lifted the matches chest high. "But you're going to have a problem soon enough."

She froze. Disbelief and horror riveted her gaze to his hands as they took out a match and then poised to strike across the black strip.

"Okay, no problems," she managed to say. "You don't have problems. I misspoke. I meant that you were in need. In need of money."

"Yeah, right. Come to you with that? You must think I'm *pupule?*"

"No, I don't think you're crazy." Just mental. Okay, maybe they were the same but she wasn't going to say so aloud. She adjusted her grip on the handle of the pitchfork. She'd get one shot and one shot only. She had to make it count.

"You'd have given me some money? Just like that?" His face twisted in skepticism.

She shifted her weight on her feet, balancing herself, preparing. *Please, Lord, help me.* "I don't know. Maybe. I mean, we could have come to some agreement."

He snorted with doubt. "No, cousin. You've come as far as you're going to."

He gestured to the floor with his chin, where a dark stain of solvent separated them. "That's the line. You can't cross."

Anticipation tightened every nerve ending Kiki possessed. Just as Pano moved to strike the match,

Kiki used all of her strength to lift and swing the pitchfork in a wide arc.

The metal prongs connected with Pano's ample shoulders, knocking the matches out of his hands and sending him sideways, crashing into the wall.

Kiki didn't hesitate. Her heart galloping, she fled, running from the shed and around the barn. As she headed toward the front yard, she heard Pano's rage-filled screams as he chased after her. She pushed herself to move faster.

As she rounded the corner, she ran smack into a wall of chest. Panic filled her brain. How had Pano made it around the other side of the building so quickly?

She struggled against the arms that held her until Ryan's voice penetrated her terror-filled mind.

"It's okay, Kiki, it's me."

Her gaze drank Ryan in as she clung to him. "You're here."

He held her close and smoothed a hand down her back. "I'm here. Are you okay?"

"Yes." She jerked back. "But Pano. He's after me."

Ryan took her face in his. "You're safe. He can't hurt you." Then he turned her around in time to see Nik leading Pano around the corner in handcuffs.

Tears filled Kiki's eyes and she buried her face into Ryan's chest. Sobs racked her body, relief and grief washed away all the fear.

Finally her tears slowed. She lifted her head to

stare into the dark eyes of the man she loved. Now seemed as good a time as any to tell him.

"Ryan, I—"

She was cut off as two EMTs surrounded them, wanting to take Kiki to their truck so they could take her to the hospital.

"Let them take care of you," Ryan insisted as she resisted going.

"You aren't leaving, are you? I mean, the island?" she asked, panicked. Would she ever get to say what was in her heart?

His tender gaze made her breath catch.

"No. I'll be right behind you."

Assured, because she knew he was a man of his word, she allowed the EMTs to transport her to the hospital.

Ryan paced the linoleum hallway of the hospital as he waited for Kiki, who was talking with her grandmother. Tutu had awakened while she had been gone, and now, Kiki was telling Tutu about Pano's arrest.

Every time Ryan thought about how close Pano had come to killing Kiki, explosions of anger erupted in his chest. He'd never been so scared in his life as when he'd found the Mercedes parked at the farm but no visible sign of her anywhere. The very real fear that Pano had kidnapped her and taken her somewhere to harm her had fired every synapse in his brain.

But some instinct had compelled Ryan to check the property. He hadn't waited for Nik's okay, but had jumped out of the cruiser and ran to the greenhouse, praying she'd be in there happily oblivious to the machinations of her cousin.

When she wasn't in the greenhouse, despair and desperation had choked him. But when he'd stepped out of the greenhouse and walked toward the barn he'd heard a sound. Not a scream exactly but a loud groan.

And then there she was, coming toward him, her head down, in an all-out run. Pano's angry bellows had given her wings. Ryan had been torn between letting Kiki keep running so he could deal with Pano himself or catching Kiki and letting her know she was safe. He'd chosen Kiki.

He would always choose Kiki.

Now he had to wait and find out if she'd choose him.

He rolled his shoulders, releasing some of the tension knotting the muscles.

"You okay?"

He spun around to find Kiki standing just a few feet from him. Closing the distance in two long strides, he wrapped her in his embrace and hugged her tight, careful of her casted arm. She squeaked and hugged him back with her good arm.

When he released her, he captured her hand. "I have something I want to say," he said, his voice sounding raw and needy.

"And I have something I want to say to you," she replied, her smile soft and almost shy.

"You first," he said, hoping she was going to say what he longed to hear from her.

"You first," she said over to him.

They shared a laugh.

He took a deep breath and then let it out. Here goes. "I've learned so much from knowing you, Kiki. You've made me realize that all the material possessions, all the wealth in the world doesn't matter compared to the relationships we form. The relationship we've formed. I know this may come out of the blue, but Kiki…I love you."

Her eyes widened and happiness spread across her face in a wide smile. "Really. I do, too." She laughed. "I mean. I love you. I love you, Ryan. And I've realized my own fears of rejection and not belonging were only preventing me from finding the happiness I know God wants for me. For us."

Joy filled his heart as he brought her fingers to his lips. He hadn't realized how scared he'd been that she wouldn't return his feelings. But now there was only love and joy and their future.

Their future.

One last hurdle to jump.

"I have a proposition for you," he said, trying to keep his anxiety from echoing in his voice.

Her smile faded to a puzzled frown. "A proposition? Like in a business deal?"

"Yes. Sort of." Oh, he was mucking this up. Just spit it out. "I want to help rebuild the farm. Only I'm thinking if we built a big house, maybe plantation style, with lots of rooms, we could turn it into a bed-and-breakfast."

"And you'd be the investor and I would run it, is that what you're saying?"

Her expression said she wasn't too keen on the idea.

"We'd run it together."

She blinked. "What?"

Disappointment roiled in his gut. "Or not. It's just a thought."

The corner of her mouth lifted and the coolness that had edged her gaze receded. "Together?"

His heartbeat picked up. He was about to commit. He was ready. "If you'll have me."

She narrowed her gaze. "What exactly are you asking?"

Duh! He'd gotten ahead of himself. Shaking his head at his own folly, he gave her a wry grin. Aware, but not caring that they were in a public setting and that anyone could watch him, he went down on one knee and took one of her hands in his. "I'm asking if you'd consider marrying me."

If the surprised bliss on her beautiful face was any indication, he anticipated a yes. His heart swelled with love and tenderness for his island girl.

She planted herself on his bent knee and linked her

good arm around his neck. He blinked in stunned pleasure.

"I accept your offer," she said, and then kissed him soundly.

EPILOGUE

December

Carrying a glass of juice, Kiki stepped out onto the ground level lanai of the beachfront rented cottage that she shared with Tutu. She took a moment to enjoy the setting sun as it danced a merry jig of reds, golds and the brightest of oranges across the calm blue waters of the Pacific Ocean. On the horizon, a cruise ship meandered past. She never tired of seeing the big white vessels floating on the blue-green water.

"Beautiful, isn't it?" Tutu commented from her spot on a lounge chair. She was still recovering from her heart attack and the doctor had ordered rest and relaxation.

"Very," agreed Ryan. He sat on the wooden porch swing, but his gaze wasn't on the view of the sunset, but on Kiki.

She beamed at him before taking the glass of POG she held to her grandmother. She had to step over Cody to reach Tutu. Cody had become Tutu's constant companion, though he still slept at the foot of Kiki's bed.

"Thank you, dear," Tutu said. "I could get used to being waited on."

Affection unfurled in Kiki's heart and she bent to kiss her grandmother's cheek. "When we get the bed-and-breakfast going, we're going to need you."

Tutu laughed. "Don't worry, I'll be ready by then."

Kiki hoped so. The construction on the ten-bedroom, plantation-style house was scheduled to be finished by next summer. She was going to need Tutu's steady presence and wonderful way with people. Kiki moved to sit beside Ryan. His arm came to drape across her shoulders. She set the swing to moving with her bare toes.

So much had happened in the past two months. Pano had been arrested and sent to jail, though the justice system would provide him with psychological counseling. Kiki still shuddered anytime she thought back to that day in the shed. She never would have guessed that her cousin was the one behind all the sabotage.

Ryan had proposed and then had to go back to Boston to settle his affairs there before returning in time to spend Thanksgiving with Kiki and Tutu, since the doctor had forbade Tutu to travel. The three of them had spent the day in quiet peacefulness.

The business model for the bed-and-breakfast was

well under way. Not only were they building a big, new house, but they would be cutting the flower crop in half to plant a lawn with a gazebo for weddings and such. And Kiki would get to concentrate on her greenhouse orchids.

Ryan had also contacted all of Horatio Lewis's investors with a new proposition to buy one of the pieces of property Kiki had shown him. A five-star resort was also under construction and Ryan had made a hefty commission.

Ryan was still living in the condo at Mana Kai. Though Kiki had a funny suspicion that Ryan had a scheme up his sleeve, because he'd kept asking her to look at wedding dresses. They weren't planning to marry until after the Kaapa Farms B and B was up and running.

She slanted him a glance, loving the way his dark wavy hair fell forward over his forehead. She couldn't resist reaching out to push the stray strands back. He caught her hand, brought the tips of her fingers to his lips before slipping a gold band with a magnificently cut diamond solitaire on to her finger.

Her breath caught. She blinked and blinked again. Her mouth opened but no words came out. Tears welled in her eyes as she turned her gaze to his.

"Do you like it?"

She nodded.

"I can take it back if you don't," he said, teasing laughter in his voice.

She hugged her hand close. "I love it. You can't have it back."

He grinned, that devastating grin that drew her in and made her melt inside. Tutu chuckled happily as she watched them. Kiki showed off the ring, loving the way the light reflected an array of colors in the cut of the diamond.

"Good. One other thing," he said, his expression turning serious. "I was hoping you'd agree to accompany me to Boston for my brother Patrick's New Year's Day wedding. Or second wedding, I should say."

Nervous excitement bubbled through her. Would his family accept her?

"If you don't want to go, I understand," he said, his gaze steady.

"But my parents will be here for Christmas." Which was a huge deal for her. They'd meet Ryan and see the plans they had for their future.

"They've agreed to stay on until we return. We can fly to Boston on December twenty-eighth and return on January third."

She grinned. "You think of everything."

"I only think of you."

Her heart swelled with love and tenderness. "New Year's in Boston sounds perfect."

"You're perfect," Ryan murmured, before he drew her close for a kiss to seal the deal.

* * * * *

Dear Reader,

Thank you for coming on this journey with Kiki and Ryan as they navigated the many facets of their relationship. They came away with a deep love for each other and a better understanding of those around them.

I hope you enjoyed the trip to the beautiful tropical paradise that is Maui. The Hawaiian Islands have a special place in my heart. My husband and I honeymooned on the lush island of Kauai and have made many trips since to Oahu and Maui. I chose Maui for this book because we recently traveled there with our children. This was their first trip, and they had a blast swimming with the sea turtles, bodysurfing and hiking through the countryside. With the setting so fresh in my mind, I just had to write Maui into a story.

May God keep watch over you always.

Aloha,

QUESTIONS FOR DISCUSSION

1. What made you pick up this book to read? Did it live up to your expectations?

2. Did you think Kiki and Ryan were realistic characters? Did their romance build believably?

3. Talk about the secondary characters. What did you like or dislike about the people in the story?

4. Was the setting clear and appealing? Could you "see" where the story took place?

5. Kiki wanted to have a place to belong. Have you ever felt that need? Why or why not? Where does that sense of belonging come from?

6. Ryan's quest to be financially secure came with a price. What was that price? What realization did he come to by the end of the story?

7. Did the suspense element of the story keep you guessing? Why or why not?

8. Did you notice the scripture in the beginning of the book? What application does it have to your life?

9. Did the author's use of language/writing style make this an enjoyable read? Would you read more from this author?

10. What will be your most vivid memories of this book?

11. What lessons about life, love and faith did you learn from this story?

12. Have you ever been in a situation where you were faced with giving up something that held great memories for you? How did you get through that time? Were you able to let go?

REQUEST YOUR FREE BOOKS!

2 FREE RIVETING INSPIRATIONAL NOVELS
PLUS 2 FREE MYSTERY GIFTS

Love Inspired
SUSPENSE

YES! Please send me 2 FREE Love Inspired® Suspense novels and my 2 FREE mystery gifts (gifts are worth about $10). After receiving them, if I don't wish to receive any more books, I can return the shipping statement marked "cancel". If I don't cancel, I will receive 4 brand-new novels every month and be billed just $4.24 per book in the U.S. or $4.74 per book in Canada, plus 25¢ shipping and handling per book and applicable taxes, if any*. That's a savings of over 20% off the cover price! I understand that accepting the 2 free books and gifts places me under no obligation to buy anything. I can always return a shipment and cancel at any time. Even if I never buy another book, the two free books and gifts are mine to keep forever.

123 IDN ERXX 323 IDN ERXM

Name	(PLEASE PRINT)	
Address		Apt. #
City	State/Prov.	Zip/Postal Code

Signature (if under 18, a parent or guardian must sign)

Order online at www.LoveInspiredSuspense.com
Or mail to Steeple Hill Reader Service:

IN U.S.A.: P.O. Box 1867, Buffalo, NY 14240-1867
IN CANADA: P.O. Box 609, Fort Erie, Ontario L2A 5X3

Not valid to current subscribers of Love Inspired Suspense books.

Want to try two free books from another series?
Call 1-800-873-8635 or visit www.morefreebooks.com

* Terms and prices subject to change without notice. N.Y. residents add applicable sales tax. Canadian residents will be charged applicable provincial taxes and GST. Offer not valid in Quebec. This offer is limited to one order per household. All orders subject to approval. Credit or debit balances in a customer's account(s) may be offset by any other outstanding balance owed by or to the customer. Please allow 4 to 6 weeks for delivery. Offer available while quantities last.

Your Privacy: Steeple Hill Books is committed to protecting your privacy. Our Privacy Policy is available online at www.SteepleHill.com or upon request from the Reader Service. From time to time we make our lists of customers available to reputable third parties who may have a product or service of interest to you. If you would prefer we not share your name and address, please check here. ☐

LISUS08R

Love Inspired®
SUSPENSE

TITLES AVAILABLE NEXT MONTH

Don't miss these four stories in October

FORSAKEN CANYON by Margaret Daley

Kit Sinclair is determined to hike through Desolation Canyon. Tribal chief of police Hawke Lonechief can't stop her, so he agrees to lead her—on *his* terms. Hawke knows the dangers the canyon holds...yet is he prepared for the stalker dogging their steps?

COUNTDOWN TO DEATH by Debby Giusti
Magnolia Medical

Five people have contracted a rare, deadly disease. It's up to medical researcher Allison Stewart to track down the source. Research is one thing—defending her life is another! Handsome recluse Luke Garrison comes to her aid. Still, with the blame for an unsolved murder hanging over Luke's head, Allison might be setting herself up to become victim number six.

A TASTE OF MURDER by Virginia Smith

A beauty pageant judge is murdered—and Jasmine Delaney could be next. She arrived in town for a wedding during the Bar-B-Q festival. But when she fills in as a pageant judge, the bride's brother, Derrick Rogers, fears she's the next target. The killer has had a taste of murder. And is hungry for more.

NOWHERE TO RUN by Valerie Hansen

Her former boyfriend told her to run...so she did. And now the thugs who killed him are after Marie Parnell and her daughter. Stuck with car trouble in Serenity, Arkansas, Marie dares to confide in handsome mechanic Seth Whitfield—who has some secrets of his own.

LISCNM0908